BRONZE JAZZ

QUID
MIRUM
PRESS™
an imprint of The Publishing Circle

BRONZE JAZZ/JOHN ALLEN MACHADO
FIRST EDITION

ISBN 978-0-9977445-7-6 (paperback)
     978-0-9977445-9-0 (hardcover)
     978-1-955018-99-9 (large print)
     978-1-955018-24-1 (eBook)

DEDICATION
For Judith

ACKNOWLEDGEMENT

I want to thank the entire team at The Publishing Circle for their guidance and patience. In 2020, my initial goal was to find a publisher who was interested in my work. What I ended up finding was Linda Stirling: a publisher, mentor, and friend. Also, writing is difficult, and putting a book together takes a lot of hard work, thought, and time. It was all worth it.

BRONZE JAZZ

John Allen Machado

ONE

JACK

I arrive hours early to catch up on dreaded paperwork. Owning the joint means I do damn near everything: bartending, hosting, mopping up puke, working as a talent scout, you name it.

I punch my code into the glowing alarm keypad and silence the obnoxious chirp-chirp-chirping. Turning away from the keypad, I instantly realize I have uninvited company. Two dark holes point directly at me. I'm slow on the uptake, my brain failing me for a prolonged second before I figure out it's a gun. A shotgun.

As I look over the gun's barrels, an inked spiderweb comes into view, sprouting from the collar of a frayed white T-shirt and covering the front of a thick, veiny neck. My eyes continue upward, landing on teardrop tattoos. Suddenly, my main goal in life is to not piss him off. I say, "Just tell me what you want."

"Open the safe."

Doing as told, I head toward the ancient safe stationed behind the bar. The room becomes a freezer, yet I find myself wiping sweaty hands on the sides of my pants. Once there, he again commands, "Open it."

I get down on unsteady knees and spin the dial. Focusing on the movement of white digits—left, right, left—I pause on the last number. Second-guessing myself, I swallow hard, hoping I got it right. I hold my breath and pull down on the gray lever as the heavy door inches open.

"The money," he demands.

I exhale and remove several deposit bags from an unlocked compartment within the safe. His gaze goes from me to the bags to the bar. Standing, I obey silent instructions and place the money on top of the bar.

Attentions are diverted as the front door unexpectedly swings opens. In walks a guy waving crumpled bills in the air. "Bartender, Johnnie Black, rocks?"

"Get the fuck out of here, you drunk motherfucker!" screams the guy with the gun.

I mumble a selfish prayer, praying that the drunkard— wearing layers of dirty clothing, silver tape binding raggedy shoes—does nothing stupid. Unfortunately, he isn't going anywhere. He looks around aimlessly, like he can't decipher where the loud insult is coming from, then returns the guy's scream with a roar of his own, "Where's my fuckin' drink?"

"I'm gonna fuckin' kill you, nigger!" shouts the crook. Raging, the Aryan-looking dude stomps out from behind the bar, swinging the shotgun in the drunk's direction.

Everything shifts into pure slow-motion as I watch the hyped-up man clear the bar. I can see his mouth moving, but I'm oblivious to the noise coming out of his pie-hole. The swing of the gun goes from high to low, back up to waist level, moving from right to left . . . but not quite there. The last thing those raised barrels point at is the outer edge of an intended target.

TWO

JACK

I snap back to real-time as four rapid-fire blasts thunder through the bar and the robber drops to the floor like a sack of potatoes. After observing the slain man, the drunk approaches me—gun at his side—and says, "What's up, Jack?"

My hands shake; I'm at a loss for words. I look at the drunk and realize I know him.

I say, "Matty," recognizing my old high school friend, Matthew Marshall. We haven't seen each other in years. He says, "You don't look so good, brother. Why don't you take a seat?"

"I can't sit right now. I'm a little fucked up and need to move. Can I fix you a drink?"

"Got anything for a hangover?" asks Matty.

"Lousy Lime Water will do the trick." Without thinking, I blurt, "You were quicker on the draw."

Matty says, "Holmes was too slow on the swing around. Plus, I executed my move more efficiently than the dead-before-he-hit-the-floor robber fuck."

Matty sips from a big glass of water while I pour a double Crown Royal, neat. I down half the glass of Canadian booze, feeling the burn as I watch blood slowly pool on the blue concrete floor. "Didn't you become a cop?" I ask.

"I did."

Matty gets up off the stool and goes over to the body, steps around the blood, then reaches down and rifles through the dead man's pockets, eventually unearthing a billfold.

"Steve Jones," he says, after flipping it open. He tosses the billfold on the guy's belly.

"Don't you have to follow certain . . ." I stop before finishing my words. Death is twenty feet away. I finally utter a complete sentence, "Shouldn't you call this in?" My next thought: *That could be me lying there.*

"No need to rush," says Matty. Adding, "I'm a detective." He smirks like something's funny, but only he gets the joke. "But I do need to call your uncle so he can see this dead peckerwood." Just the mention of the word "uncle" makes me agitated as all get-out.

In an instant, my intuition kicks into high gear as I turn back the clock a decade or so to a suicide note left for my eyes only. A note that warned me about my uncle. I didn't take the warning seriously, though, because I was young and dumb with little to lose but naivete. Do I now have something to worry about?

In less than ten minutes, in walks the number-two man for the SFPD, my uncle, David O'Shea—the very same man I was warned about—accompanied by three guys in dark suits sporting identical cop haircuts.

Matty looks at me and whispers, "Be cool." After a quick wink, he gets off the barstool and approaches my uncle. They walk to the back of the bar and stand next to the stage, distancing themselves from the rest of us. Without shaking hands or exchanging pleasantries, they have a brief, hushed conversation before Matty does an about-face and heads toward the front entrance. He weaves his way around tables and chairs before reaching a pair of my uncle's minions. They appear mesmerized as they gawk at the dead guy. Matty glances my way and gives me a slight nod before nudging past the last cop standing guard at the door. As Matty leaves, I feel desperately alone.

"How've you been, Jack?" asks my uncle, shifting his gaze up and away from the man on the floor as he walks over to the dark cherrywood bar. I reach for the bottle and pour more Crown Royal, taking a quick drink as he approaches. My uncle extends his hand.

"Been better," I say, reaching across the bar to get on with the formalities. Then I turn into something I detest, regressing back to childhood, as I nod the correct nods and contort my face in just the right way, replying with the occasional "absolutely" and "definitely" while looking directly into my uncle's eyes and posing as the attentive listener. When my uncle finishes with his nonsensical diatribe and a few not-so-subtle threats as to who I should and shouldn't associate with, starting with Joseph Rosenbaum, my business partner—like I can avoid that arrangement—I end the conversation with yet another handshake and a lie. "I will make a serious effort to heed your advice, sir." Yes, I actually end my lie with "sir."

Stymied by fear, I avoid asking the obvious: Why are you suddenly back in my life giving unwanted advice? Why the threats? Heck, we've maybe seen each other three times in the last ten years, at unavoidable family events—funerals, weddings, christenings—where less than a handful of words were exchanged.

As I ponder the current situation, including my lack of courage, my uncle walks away with two of his flunkeys in tow, appearing satisfied that what needed to be done got done, that what needed to be said got said. As he pushes through the door, he stops and turns my way, saying, "The investigative team will be in and out of here in no time. After the coroner removes this worthless stiff, the crime scene cleanup crew will take care of the rest."

I follow him to the door at a comfortable distance, intending to lock it behind him, just as an unmarked police cruiser pulls up to the curb. As I watch him walk away, it smacks me even harder—it makes no sense that he was here.

A new thought crosses my mind: I need to have a serious conversation with the slick and winking Matthew Marshall, the detective that has what I don't—balls the size of California cantaloupes.

THREE

JACK

Sean O'Shea was a beautiful baby, over time becoming a beautiful young man. Everything a guy wanted to be. Personality? He had it. Looks? Already mentioned them. Athletic? Very much so. Sean O'Shea was also my best friend and cousin.

We grew up in San Francisco, out in the avenues, what the tourists and transplants call the Sunset District. His dad and my dad were brothers and third-generation San Franciscans. Black Irish, the two O'Shea brothers. My mom: Norwegian. His: Sicilian. Sean's mixed bloodline resulted in this velvety bronze skin, skin that was utterly remarkable. Made you want to taste it, like licking warm cinnamon toast. I've only seen skin like his on one other person and she was a combination of different bloodlines altogether, but still that same gorgeous skin.

We did everything together. Well, almost everything. At nineteen, Sean took a dive off the Golden Gate Bridge.

I wasn't invited.

Nobody saw that coming. Not even me.

His suicide changed a few family dynamics. It definitely changed me. My dad died when I was twelve, but I welcomed his death. He was a bully and a prick and a physical abuser. His death brought relief. With Sean, though, that death hurt.

The word on the street, as well as with the police, was that he hadn't left a suicide note. Most everyone thought this to be true. But it wasn't. Sean left a note—a letter, really—and he left it for me to find. Which I did. I decided not to share it with anybody else—didn't quite see the point in doing that.

A writer for one of San Francisco's free weekly newspapers, *The City Wrap*, captured Sean's final moments with eloquence, writing: *Several eyewitnesses said that a beautiful young man, shedding all clothing as he strolled along the bridge walkway, climbed over the railing and flew into the morning sky—angelic-like—with a look on his face that made them want to cry. And cry they did.*

I saved the article. It moved me. Regardless of the subject matter, the words put down on paper simply rang true, the essence of what really happened right there in black and white.

The day Sean died brought commotion on the street where we lived, especially across the street and four houses down. That day's theme: police cars everywhere, with comings and goings into the night and the following day's early morning hours. The O'Shea brothers—one dead, one alive—had chosen the profession of San Francisco Irish cop, and the Irish cop gang loves to show support for a fellow cop, especially when that cop wields power.

Sensing something amiss, my mom and I hustled down to my uncle's house and were quickly hit in the face with the unthinkable. My uncle pulled me aside and asked if I was all right. "No," I said, tears streaming down my cheeks. He then went into a bullshit fatherly interrogation to see if I knew why

Sean committed suicide, in the end asking, "Did Sean leave you a note or say anything?"

I just stared at him, my typical response when asked questions I don't have answers to. He finally let up, pouring two fingers of Irish whiskey into a tumbler and handing it to me, saying everything was going to be fine. Then he walked away and joined the cop gang for more drinking and speculating . . . definitely no crying. But things were not "fine," with death being final and all.

Sipping whiskey, I thought about the secret hiding spots Sean and I had kept since childhood. Places where we shared private stuff like miniature liquor bottles, ragweed joints, ticket stubs, insulting notes, risqué Irish limericks, stolen packs of cigarettes, various magazines and comic books and puzzles, and a wide assortment of other useless shit. His secret spot rested in their backyard shed in an old metal bucket stored way up high. My secret spot sat above our garage in the attic, inside a sturdy cardboard box.

I downed the whiskey, wanting badly to flee the surrounding uncomfortableness. After finding my mom in the kitchen, I gave her a hug and excused myself and hustled home. I went directly to the attic. Bingo. Sean's letter.

I didn't read it at first, wanting to take it somewhere other than the house, the attic. A deep need to be alone and unbothered drove me, as I feared my reaction to the unknown. Off I went to the beach, the letter folded and stuffed in my jacket pocket.

Sean and I had been together at Ocean Beach the day before he died. Out in the cold water, body surfing. Only strong swimmers venture into the tricky surf at Ocean Beach, with its undertows, currents, and large winter waves. Two hours out in the chilled water was enough. Later, we split a monster burrito at a nearby taco truck before walking home. We hadn't made plans to hang out the following day.

Sean had other plans.

In retrospect, there was nothing odd or different about our final time together. It was simply us enjoying us—in the ocean, in the moment. We'd immersed ourselves in familiar smells lingering through the air: neoprene, human sweat, wet dogs, roasting coffee, highway exhaust, and simmering food-truck food. I hadn't seen signs of anything out of the ordinary. Lesson learned: realities and perceptions can quickly change.

Sitting in the sand, I looked out at the breaking waves and centered myself. I'd chosen an isolated spot, far from the wet, packed sand to avoid the walkers, the runners, the loiterers. Unfolding the letter, I mentally braced myself. I read slowly, taking in every word, pausing at every comma, and stopping at each period. Paying attention to what was written. Then, I read it again. And a third time. The contents of the letter shocked me yet helped me understand Sean's reasoning.

I failed him. I should've known, and not knowing was just a poor excuse.

I don't think suicide would have been my choice, but I hadn't experienced what he'd experienced. Truth told; I don't know what I would've done.

At the end of his letter, he'd scribbled an overt warning: *Destroy this after you've read it. Don't tell another living soul. He will kill to keep secrets hidden. He will crush you and everything you love.*

No wonder I'd been blindsided earlier with questions from his father.

Sean loved life and that love of life radiated outward. He loved the ocean, jazz, all kinds of food (including Zingers by the dozen), too many books to count, socialism, the concept of a higher power, and, most important to us both, the San Francisco Giants and baseball in general. Pretty much everything I loved, except for a few too-deep-for-me subjects and higher powers. However, he gave it all up that winter morning.

I tucked his letter back in my jacket.

Sean's funeral arrived before I knew it. I wasn't ready. Who could be? A full Catholic mass spilled over to a wake at the house—an eating, drinking spectacle running late into the night, with the eating part playing second fiddle to the drinking part.

Prior to my departure, maybe midway through the wake, I spent an unplanned couple of minutes alone with my Aunt Maddie. For the briefest of moments, we had an awkward discussion about Sean. She fumbled her words, as did I—as if actual truths should be kept at a distance. Then she let me know they were selling the house and moving to another part of the city: Noe Valley.

No surprise. Why stick around with all the memories of Sean in this house? In this neighborhood? Too many memories, so get the hell out.

As I started to leave, my uncle guided me out to the sidewalk for a brief conversation. Boasting, he told me if I ever found myself in trouble, or in need of anything, anything at all, I should reach out and ask him for help. He said he could assist me in ways I couldn't imagine. In the end, he said I could tell him anything—that it would stay between us. Only us. He'd never spoken to me like this, and I wasn't sure what he was getting at.

I never liked either of the O'Shea brothers. A dead father

meant one problem solved. Keeping a healthy distance from my uncle was how I planned to deal with him. I could act sideways at times if I truly wanted something, or if I needed to save my ass. For some reason, though, I could never muster the courage to stand up to either of them. I reeked of cowardice.

But I wasn't like the two O'Shea brothers in that I could be honest with myself when it came to my own selfish pursuits. They always seemed oblivious to their fucked up, manipulative ways. As my uncle's one-sided conversation wound down, he reached out and shook my hand. "You're a fine lad," he said, in the slightest Irish brogue. Typical drunk Irish American trying to sound old-country Irish, but not coming close.

Off I went to the ocean, accompanied by a half pint of whiskey and a can of Stout, definitely another Irish Catholic American lad in the city of many. Once I found the right spot—the place where I'd last spent time with Sean—I got naked, piling clothes on top of my drink to conceal the treasure. Shivering, I waded into the ocean for a night swim and to reflect on Sean.

The frigid saltwater had its effect on my body. I swam past the break and made my way out about a quarter mile or so. I felt alive in the ever-cold water, the soft undulation of an ocean swell lifting then gently setting me back down. Treading water for several minutes, I focused on the good times with Sean . . . which turned out to be most of the time spent with him. Finally, I dove into darkness, down about twenty feet, my ears popping due to increased pressure.

Mentally challenging myself, I stayed down a beat or two too long, an eerie moment of faith, blind in the elements, waiting for an internal hint that oxygen was required. At last, I forcefully exhaled and vigorously kicked and kicked and kicked while aching for the relief of a full breath. Surfacing, I gulped the crisp night air.

I spun a three-sixty and looked around the ocean top. I hung out for another couple of minutes before beginning the swim back to shore, all the while wondering what predators lurked below. I thought, *Which predators are worse? The ones in the ocean or the ones on land?* I didn't much fear the ones beneath me. I respected them, more than anything. Without a doubt, I feared the human kind.

Making it back to shore with shriveled cock and balls, I hustled into my clothes and sat down in the cool sand, happy that thieving vagrants hadn't stolen my bottle, my can, my clothes. I took a long pull on the green bottle and felt the burn as I swallowed. I popped the can of Murphy's, chasing whiskey with lukewarm beer. The wonderful combination of spirits made me feel warm, invincible, sad. I sat there for quite some time, sipping and thinking. Just before sunrise, I walked home. It was time to reconsider things and get some much-needed sleep.

I dreamt of Sean often that first year after his death, dreams where he'd suddenly appear. They felt real. Eventually those dreams faded as life moved on. My thoughts of Sean became fewer and fewer. The pain didn't seem so near.

But I never forgot why he did what he did . . . and who pushed him over the brink.

FOUR

JACK

Time moves on, but my mind does not. Why had Uncle David been informed of a robbery at a bar in the city, regardless of my relationship with him? And why was he, a high-ranking big shot, available to respond so quickly at such an early morning hour, his lackeys following close behind, all showered and neatly groomed? Why had I been told by my uncle to be careful about my relationship—my friendship and partnership—with Joseph Rosenbaum? Did that admonition have something to do with the bar, or could it be with the fact that Joseph owns *The City Wrap*—an influential local paper? My head spins with a boatload of questions as I watch the cleanup crew do the final mop-up of the concrete floor.

Just as the crew is getting ready to exit, the front door swings open and Ana Gonzalez—our general manager—hustles through. Looking back at unfamiliar faces and then in my direction, she asks, "What's up?"

"Got robbed."

"You all right?"

"A little less than all right."

We've been friends and workmates for years, spending long stretches of time together. She understands me better than most. Ana gives me the up and down while approaching the bar and popping up to sit on a barstool. "Give me the gory details. If you leave anything out, Isabella won't be working here anymore."

Isabella, Ana's eleven-year-old daughter, who happens to be deaf, has been my business protégé for a couple of years.

My quick reply: "Extortion won't be necessary, Miss Overreaction."

I begin my tale of robbery, death, and the accompanying family-related surprises. Twenty minutes later, I slap the bar top with an open hand and say, "That's about it," as I continue to view Ana's face for any signs of questions or utter disbelief regarding my oratory dramatics. She isn't saying much, nor exhibiting any obvious odd facial expressions. Ana simply says, "Wow," followed by a "huh" before she stands up and walks away, apparently transitioning into work mode and readying herself for another week of fine dining, bar activity, and jazz adventure at The Hall.

An hour later and nearly in tears—I suppose she's fully processed what I told her—Ana corners me in the back next to the bullpen and says, "Do you understand what this place means to me and Isabella and Roberto?"

She looks away, her head angled toward a side wall, then turns back to say, "I love you. Isabella loves you. Roberto doesn't love you, but he likes you a lot and even trusts you. That's it, my official rant."

She pivots and walks towards the kitchen doors, pushing through, leaving me to watch swinging doors swing. Seconds later, she peeks around the outer edge of one of the doors and says, "By the way, I made a call to you-know-who." Having said her piece, she vanishes.

I watch as Ana disappears. The Hall is a huge part of our lives and I want that to continue. I will do my darndest to ensure everyone's safety. But first, I have to deal with my mentor, the "who" part of the "you-know-who" equation.

The post-lunch drinking crowd starts to flow in just as Joseph Rosenbaum marches through the front door. He's wearing a navy-blue blazer with a crisp, cobalt-blue, button-down dress shirt, impeccably pressed khaki pants, and his signature retro-gray New Balance walking shoes. He has three or four different variations of this "uniform" as I call it, a different colored button-down shirt and off-colored khaki pants, all similar and always with the same shoes.

"Hey, Professor," I call out as I pour drinks. After wrapping things up with a few customers, I walk down to meet him at the far end of the bar.

Joseph goes by a lot of names because he wears a variety of hats: Professor, boss, Mr. Rosenbaum, Big Joe, The Jew (complimentary or derogatory, depending on who is saying it and how they're saying it), Rosy, and a few other choice monikers. The Professor looks me squarely in the eyes, and says, "What the hell's going on?"

"You heard the news."

"Yes, I got wind of the robbery. Allen Smith is coming down here later this afternoon to do a story so we can get out in front of whatever's behind all this nonsense."

"It's really weird, Professor. Everything happened like it was prearranged. The robbery, the killing, and my uncle showing up. The quick investigation, the body removal, the cleanup."

"Hmm," he says. "Let's say it's nothing—even though it stinks of *something*—then it'll be just another armed robbery with a happy ending for the law enforcement gang."

"You really think there's something to it?"

Rosy shoots his cuffs, still standing a short distance from the bar, not wanting to muss pristine clothing by taking a seat or touching a dirty surface. A glass falls off a nearby table, shattering on the concrete floor. I stuff my initial reaction to run over and take care of it. Let the waitstaff handle it.

I look back at Rosy and he sneers at me, as if to say, *We're having a conversation here.*

He regains my attention. "Of course I think there's something to it. But I get it. You don't know what to do about it. And I'm telling you not to worry about that, Jack. Together we'll figure it out. However, your uncle and his people, if that's what we're going to call them, are behind this. Smith knows what to ask and how to form the story. Whether it turns out to be big or not, well, we'll just have to wait and see."

He takes a quick peek at his watch, looks back at me, and says, "Right now, I've got work to do. If anything out of the ordinary happens, call me ASAP. If I'm not at the office, someone will get a message to me. Take care. Oh, and don't speak with any reporters except Smith."

With that, he turns and heads for the exit. I call after him, "You take care too, Professor."

Loudly clearing her throat from the opposite end of the bar, Ana yells, "Did I do the right thing?"

"What do you think?" I can't help but smile at her. "When is Isabella getting here?"

"Around three is what she told me. Why don't you text her?"

"I thought they weren't supposed to have electronic gizmos on at school," I reply, as I head for the kitchen to retrieve my cell phone.

"You're the one who bought her that electronic gizmo thingy. And you're right, they're not supposed to have them on, but they do."

I half listen because my mind is drifting elsewhere, letting me know the answers to my questions have yet to unfold.

22

JOHN ALLEN MACHADO

FIVE

JACK

At two minutes past three, Isabella and Roberto appear. A few regulars wave to Isabella as her eyes adjust in dim lighting. Once she notices her admirers, she waves back—seemingly embarrassed, yet happy to be recognized. Roberto is not her biological father, but you'd never know it.

"Hey gunslinger," Roberto says to me.

I smile at Isabella and nod at Roberto. Isabella heads for the kitchen—a shortcut to the backroom—to tend to the cold brew as Roberto walks over and gives Ana a kiss.

Leaving Roberto and Ana to themselves, I follow Isabella. She high-fives our chef, then his assistant, Carlos, before exiting the kitchen into the much cooler storage room. I tap her on the shoulder and dart to the other side as the smell of coffee grows stronger. Not surprised in the least, she reacts to my overused, silly gesture by turning and facing me while rolling her eyes. She can speak and read lips, and once I figured out her speech patterns, her tones, her cadence, we transitioned into a simple form of communication that feels natural.

She can sign. I can't. However, I quickly learned the characters of the alphabet. So, when she signs to me, she signs as if sending a text message: LOL, WTF, and so on. Our own acronym-speak, with few others the wiser.

Isabella signs, "WH?"

I tell her what happened, giving her a medium-speed, concise overview of the robbery and shooting and my uncle showing up. She signs, "TFC."

Her way of saying, "That's fucking crazy." I've never treated her like a child. She's more a business partner and friend.

Isabella signs, "LGOWI," and I say, "Yeah, let's get on with it."

Isabella begins to pull the rubber stoppers on the containers holding coffee, coffee that's been soaking in water for over a day. While the coffee drains through special wool filters invented by some Ivy League dude in the 1960s, she prepares labels with exact dates and times while I retrieve the twenty-seven-ounce, narrow, cylindrical glass bottles—sleeves as we call them—from ratty cardboard boxes positioned on the same countertop as the draining black liquid.

I taught Isabella my version of the cold brew process and the importance of a twenty-four-hour soak. I also taught her a second cold brew recipe, aptly named "dirty brew", where the filtering system is a bright red automotive funnel with a fine mesh screen at the exit hole. This allows for a fine sediment to reach the brew. Some of the hardcore cold brew aficionados think the dirty brew has a more intense flavor than its counterpart. The two of us alone control the cold brewing process, preparing and monitoring it six days a week. Only we know the true recipe: the coffee to water ratio, the preferred fair-trade coffees used, and most important of all, which water is used and where it's sourced. The final product is a coffee concentrate that is strong as fuck—much stronger than a typical cup of coffee or a shot of espresso. Those who consume it usually dilute it with milk or water, or a combination of both.

"This shit is art," I tell Isabella.

She shakes her head and signs, "TSR!" *This shit rocks!*

With the new consignment of brew near completion, I push through the swinging doors and head out to the bar, leaving Isabella to fend for herself as she begins to make a batch of Lousy Lime Water. The secret behind the water is, of course, the water . . . and the amount of fresh-squeezed lime juice added to each half-gallon growler. Even though it is not a complicated process, it is an exact process that also has to be properly labeled and dated for accurate stock rotation. Like the coffee—first made, first used—the Lousy Lime Water quantities have to be sufficient because of high sales volume. The patrons at The Hall love their cold brew, their lime water, their booze.

I motion to Ana and shout, "Meet me in the office." We're on a tight timeline and need to get bands scheduled. Jazz is the loosely suggested genre of music usually performed here. However, the bands who've auditioned in the past haven't always fit that mold. In truth, we look for talented musicians who can play. Ana and I try for an eclectic mix of talent. If we disagree, or aren't sure about a specific band or musician, then Mike Gates, our Lithuanian chef, is brought into the mix to determine whether we should give them an opportunity or not.

Mike Gates is not his real name. His given Lithuanian name is too difficult to pronounce, or, as Mike Gates likes to say, "Americans with mind narrow butcher my name often times." So, Mike Gates is the name he chose, and he insists that he be called by both his first and last name. Not Mike. Not Gates. Not Mr. Gates. Nothing other than Mike Gates. When we leave it to Mike Gates, he consistently picks tight, solid acts that put on well-remembered performances. He often reminds us, "I pick band Frozen Monkey before anybody knew that monkey."

Finished with band selections for the month, Ana and I head back out to the bar to check on sales and inventory numbers. Halfway through counting bottles of booze, I look up from my clipboard just as Detective Matthew Marshall glides into The Hall. I introduce him to Ana, saying, "Meet the killer."

Matty ignores my introduction and shakes Ana's hand.

"You're just the man I wanted to see," I tell him. "I would like to speak with you at length after I leave this fine establishment tonight."

"Cool," is Matty's one-word reply. "Could I get a jug of that Lousy Lime Water to go?"

Ana says, "You're hooked. I'll get you a growler. It's on the house for saving Jack's ass."

"Thank you, young lady," says Matty, turning on the charm.

As Ana walks away, Matty and I agree on a time and place to meet later on. I need some answers.

SIX

JACK

Just as Ana hands Matty a growler, I notice Allen Smith, a writer for *The City Wrap,* hunched over at the bar. Caught up in the day-to-day, I never saw him come in.

Smith does his nightly drinking—five, six nights a week—at The Hall. It strikes me as odd that as often as I've seen him over the years, I still don't know much about the stocky, tough looking, heavy-drinking man. Walking behind the bar, I snatch a fifth of Don Julio Anejo off the top shelf, open it, and pour generous shots into a couple of shot glasses before taking them over to Smith. Parked on a stool at mid bar, Smith acknowledges me with barely a tilt of the head, downs a shot of the smooth tequila, grabs the other, and sips the tiniest of sips before placing it back on the bar. After a brief pause, he finally looks up and asks a question he already knows the answer to. "Wasn't that the killer cop who just left?"

"Do you mean the detective who saved my life this morning?"

Smith smiles, downs the second shot of tequila, and says, "This morning's killing was the seventh time in a three-year period that detective Matthew Marshall has killed another human being while on the job."

"Really?"

"Yeah, really. He's been a cop for eight years, and in the last three years, while working for David O'Shea, he's shown a certain tendency for killing folks. The five years prior, he never fired his weapon in the line of duty except during target practice at the city range. I'd call that a pattern."

I'm caught off-guard, having never really had a conversation with Smith. As much as he writes, he's a keep-it-close-to-the-vest dude. I finally say, "Matty's an old friend."

"If I were you, I'd rethink some of my friend and family choices." He stands up, saying, "Mother Nature's calling. Can I get two more shots of the DJ Anejo with a Lousy Lime Water back?"

"No problem," I reply to his back as he lumbers toward the john.

Once Smith returns, he stands there, staring at me before finally saying, "Things are going to get ugly with this story. Your uncle doesn't like the paper, me, Rosy, or what we represent. Just so you know, I'm not a big fan of David O'Shea, either."

He finally grabs a seat, adjusts his ass on the barstool, and continues. "I'm going to squash all those bad feelings and do my job, get the facts, play dirty if I have to, and sleep with a gun under my pillow in case your uncle decides to sic one of his hired killers on me. If you think I'm paranoid, or that I drink too much, which I do, then I would have to look you straight in the eyes and tell you that you are one naive young man."

Smith again sips at his drink. I keep my mouth shut, my silence nudging him on. "Rosy mentioned that you've been avoiding that uncle of yours for some time. I'm guessing you trust him about as far as you can throw him into the Pacific Ocean with lead weights tied around his nuts. Aside from everything I just said, he's not such a bad guy, the piece of crap that he is and all."

I again watch as Smith downs another shot of tequila before taking a long pull on the Lousy Lime Water.

"For sure, my uncle doesn't fit the mold of, as you put it, 'not such a bad guy.' He's a hundred times worse. But even though Matty works for my uncle, he's still my friend. He didn't hesitate to save my life this morning. And that counts for something, whether you think it does or not. By the way, those drinks are on the house."

"Looks like you and I will have to agree to disagree on a few tender points. But remember this—what we discuss stays between us. You don't tell your uncle squat about what's going to hit the papers. Deal with Marshall any way you see fit."

Smith reaches out and claps a heavy hand on my shoulder. "But don't be stupid. If you let something slip that you shouldn't let slip, you'd better let me know about it. I protect my sources because they put a lot of trust in me. What I'm saying is, be smart and trust the people that you really trust and nobody else. Got it?"

"You're right, we don't agree on everything. Now, what do you need from me?"

"Answers to a few questions. I already have the bulk of what I need to stir the pot of shit and get the right people's attention over at City Hall." Smith looks down the bar at a couple readying to leave. Lifting an empty glass in my direction, he says, "Since you're buying, can I get two more shots of the DJ Anejo?"

We continue going over details of the robbery. It doesn't

take long before I'm officially tired of hearing myself talk.

Smith spends an hour or so with me before he heads to wherever dedicated journalists go. He doesn't even seem buzzed after downing six shots of tequila.

Suddenly, I want to take my words back—every single one of them—because of the overpowering fear associated with my uncle's future scrutiny.

SEVEN

JACK

I depart The Hall at ten that night, making a beeline for my apartment. I live on the top floor of an eleven-story building that Rosenbaum owns. It also houses the headquarters of *The City Wrap*. The first two floors are dedicated to the weekly rag, and the building's lighted sign—looming large on its façade—makes that apparent.

THE CITY WRAP
THE TRUTH CHRONICLED

After meeting Matty outside, we enter and stroll toward the elevator, then ascend to the divided top floor. I live on the side that overlooks Union Square. Rosenbaum's apartment sets opposite mine and offers a wider view of the city. A lobby separates the two.

"Nice digs," says Matty, looking around. "Lacking in furniture, but still, nice digs."

As we walk into the wide-open space of the storage-room-turned-flat, what unfolds to the eye is a row of white cement pillars—four in total, thick in diameter, twenty feet in height.

The only walls, the perimeter walls, match the pillars in color and height. Most everything else is in plain view: bathtub/ shower/sink located at the far end, tall black stereo speakers precisely distanced and angled at the center of the apartment, a two-compartment stainless steel sink off to the right, and, to my left, a library's share of books lining multiple shelves spanning at least a third of the apartment. Out of view is the toilet, positioned in the far-left corner, hidden behind thick canvas drapes that extend from ceiling to floor and then some.

"What we're standing in used to be the building's storage space. Rosy put me in charge of the remodeling project. Said if I did a good job, I could move in. This is the result."

"So, the Jew owns this building. Smart man and a dangerous man."

"Dangerous?"

"The power of the pen, the paper it's printed on, and money and influence to back it all up," replies Matty.

"Good point. You want a drink?" I motion towards an expensive bottle of booze. He nods, affirming that the thirty-year-old Islay Scotch will do just fine.

We settle into the only two chairs in the apartment and sip peaty scotch. Matty begins, saying, "So what's on your mind?"

I get right to the point. "Wanted to ask you what my uncle is really up to. What the robbery was all about. Why you conveniently showed up to save my ass. Why you've killed seven people since you began working for my uncle and zero before that. Do I need to fear my uncle? Do I need to do anything about him?"

"That's a lot of questions. Let me see if I can help you out. First of all, I won't be working for your uncle as of tonight. We're meeting at Ocean Beach at midnight and I'm going to ask for and receive a transfer. What went down this morning wasn't planned. At least not on my end. I had no clue that crazy white boy was going to show up." Matty takes a sip of whiskey and looks into the glass, swirling the liquid round and round before answering. "Did David know? I'm sure he did. That said, we are lucky to be alive. As far as me discharging my firearm in the line of duty, let's just say I've been put into some precarious positions by your uncle that have resulted in a few folks dying. It was either me or them. All justified. By the way, this conversation stays between me and you and not your writer friend. Agreed?"

I conclude that he saw Allen Smith at the bar earlier, just like Smith had spotted him. *My friend*, I scoff inwardly before saying, "Agreed."

"Cool. Also, I showed up because your uncle ordered me to be there. Told me to go deep undercover so as not to get recognized. I guess he wanted to keep it on the low. I've been watching you for over a week. Your uncle spun it as a favor to him just to make sure everything was cool with you at The Hall. I didn't believe that at the time, and I certainly don't believe it now. Your uncle has bigger plans in this city than just being the number two guy on the force. For some reason he doesn't trust you or the Jew and you two seem to be connected at the hip." Matty pauses and asks, "Did I answer all your questions?"

"I think so. But I have a couple more." I reach for the bottle to top off his drink. Matty puts a hand over his glass and I ease back in my chair.

"Are you going to be safe in the middle of the night? Seriously, what gives with that?"

"I'll be more than safe. Ocean Beach is your uncle's thinking, scheming, outside office. It's where he winds down with a cigar at the end of a long day after doing what it is men like him do. You know, mental positioning for loftier things in our fine city, as well as sweating the past. One never knows what might pop up and squash an ascent for power. Your uncle is one smart, conniving cat."

"I don't know what to do, exactly."

"You'll figure it out. You're a big boy, Jack. But if you have any questions, ask the right people. Like me."

"Can I trust you?"

Matty looks directly at me, smiles, and says, "You'll have my full support after midnight. I'll be in touch." With that, he stands, downs his drink, hands me the empty glass, and walks out of the apartment. I follow to shut the door. Once he's in the lobby, he stops and turns.

"Hey, I noticed you don't have live music at The Hall on Sundays."

Although not expecting that comment, I don't miss a beat. "I take it you want to help me out with that. I didn't know you were a talent scout and a quick-on-the-draw cop all rolled into one."

Matty gives me a *fuck you* look and extends both hands above his shoulders—a preacher at the pulpit ready to convince his flock. "I have a cousin, my mom's brother's daughter. I think that makes her my first cousin or something like that. Anyway, she just happens to play jazz and classical piano and can sing some, too. She's been in the city for a couple of years now. Moved here from New Mexico. Thought maybe you could give her an audition. Let her play on Sundays if you think her classical training is up to snuff. Maybe play for an hour or two. Mellow stuff. Easy hangover music. Her daddy was the man-about-town back in the day when the Fillmore was jumping."

"Send her by next Wednesday morning around nine. We'll

give her a listen. See what she's got."

"I'll do that," replies Matty. "Her name is Jasmine. She spells it like the flower and not like a stripper from the Hood. Oh, and she's classy, too. So treat her right."

"She's your family. Of course I'll treat her right. I wouldn't want to have to deal with her cousin. I hear he has a tendency to kill people when they rub him the wrong way."

EIGHT

JASMINE

Shortly after walking in, I sense something is off. As I sit down at the kitchen table, watching as he shuts and locks the front door, I know I've made a mistake. I should bolt, run like a wild animal. Too late.

My ears ring as I stagger from the dingy house, my eyes slowly adjusting to the glaring sun. The taste and smell of iron is from my own blood. I'm sore and hurt; sore and hurt in all the wrong places, especially my sense of worth.

I'm eighteen and not a virgin anymore. I've had sex before, but never forced or unwanted. Mama warned me. *Don't go over to Uncle Russell's house when he's been drinking. Don't go there at all unless you're with me.* I didn't think he'd be drinking on a Sunday morning. I thought I'd stop by after my piano lesson to say hi, just to see how he was doing.

I can't get home fast enough. Eager as I am, I stop and puke—splattering my shoes, puddling on the dry desert floor. Fluid runs down my face, a mixture of snot, vomit, and tears.

I need Mama. I need to take a shower, followed by a long soak in the tub.

To see me, to smell me, is to know something bad has happened. Mama sees, dropping garden shears in her wake, running. She holds me tight and I whisper his name. She guides me toward the house. My fingers touch familiar, textured walls. Safe walls. Home.

Mama can't stop saying she's sorry and that she loves me. She's gentle as she bathes me. I thank her. I tell her what happened.

Tears stream down her weathered face. A strong face . . . but not right now. *We'll see Doc in the morning*, she says. I'm finally warm and safe. Mama continues her gentle ways. I get into Mama's big old bed. Clean skin on crisp, cool sheets. She gets in with me and holds me and cries some more and again tells me she loves me. "I love you too, Mama," I say.

Doc swings by the next day. A house call on the rez is not the norm. Mama called in a favor. The doc has everything she needs in a bright red Craftsman toolbox. She takes my blood to be tested for sexually transmitted diseases, all of them, especially the ones that kill. Doc gives me a morning-after pill, just in case. Seems like his baby would be far worse than a disease. Diseases, not so bad. Possibility of life from him, disastrous.

Like Mama, Doc is full-on indigenous. Not Pueblo, but some tribe from the desert side of Oregon. She's cool, and she's stuck around longer than we thought she would. She loves my music. Mama and I love her. She's gentle, treating me with dignity and letting me know when things are going to hurt or be uncomfortable. She says I'll recover, that I'll heal up just fine. No future problems. However, Doc's concerned about my mental state, as is Mama. Me too. I need time, space, isolation in the desert. I need to play the piano.

The itching related to healing begins the day after Doc's exam. To physically recover is just that: the beginning of an itch, from sore to itch, to being less sore, to more itch, to a little sore, to a little less itch, to forgetting you were ever injured, even though you were. The mental violation takes more time.

But at some point, alone in the desert, it dawns on me that I don't hate my uncle anymore. I'll never see him again, or give validation to his violation, or care about him at all. The hate part fades, and eventually he fades away, too. Freedom.

"Mama, what are you going to do?" I ask one late summer day as we husk ears of corn in the kitchen, two months before I plan to leave New Mexico.

"Please don't worry none, young lady. You look so good. You're yourself again. I'm happy you decided to get out of here. You go out to that big city and play piano just like your papa did. Don't forget the letter he wrote you before he passed."

"My validation."

"That's right. So go be what you are. A jazzwoman."

"I will, Mama, but I'm a little scared. I don't know if I'm good enough."

"You're supposed to be scared. That's life. You are good enough, but the only way you'll get that resolved in your head is by playing for people in the big city, and I don't mean Albuquerque. You have an auntie who loves you and has been writing to you and me since you were born. She took a bus ride out to Albuquerque when you were just a baby. She came out here with her mother—your papa's mother, your grandmother—so they could see you and hold you and let you know you had family in San Francisco. Now she wants to give you a fresh start."

"Does she know what happened?"

"Baby, I've told you a few times now that what happened is between me, you, him, and the doc. That dies with the four of us. What she does know is that you want to play piano in the city where your papa first got recognized as a great musician."

"Thanks, Mama. I want to make you proud."

"You already have."

NINE

JASMINE

I set out for San Francisco on a Greyhound bus three days after my nineteenth birthday. Crying, I already miss my mama. Mama cried, too, tears streaming down her face as she stood in the deserted parking lot watching the bus drive away. Like my father, I've made up my mind: I am going to be a jazzman . . . a jazzwoman.

I arrive at The City By The Bay on a breezy fall day. Waiting for me at the station are my Auntie Anne—my papa's little sister—and her son, my cousin Matthew. They're there to give me a family greeting, a loving greeting. On the drive home, they talk about my father like he was the man about town. Apparently he was, back in the day in what they refer to as the Fillmore. I don't know anything about the Fillmore, but I feel proud to hear my papa's kin talk about him the way they do, as if speaking of royalty.

"He made it a point to help his family, his people," says Auntie Anne as we arrive at her house in Potrero Hill.

I can feel my papa's presence as I prepare myself to stand where he stood and walk where he walked. Anne explains that my papa came out to San Francisco from Missouri when he was fifteen. He came to live with his grandmother, my great-grandmother. Over time, he brought the rest of the family from Kansas City, supporting them until they could make their own way.

As I walk through the door, there in the first room, shiny and bright, sets my papa's old upright piano. Anne looks at me and says, "That was your papa's favorite piano and he asked me to keep it in fine condition for you."

Tears well and fall as I step over and touch the spotless instrument. I glance back at Anne. It's a day for teardrops.

Matthew rolls his eyes and says, "Play something, girl. I've heard your discs, now let me hear you live. Go on now."

I sit on the sturdy wooden bench, slowly lifting the cover and unveiling the keys. I can feel Papa looking over my shoulder and saying, "Play me something nice, baby. Sweet and slow." I rest my fingers on the keys, inhale the scent of another generation, and begin playing a Thelonious Monk tune, a number any jazzman would know. The whispers flow from my family members' mouths, "Damn girl", "Oh, yeah", and "Play that", "Uh huh", "Sweet Jesus", "Nice."

I play like I was taught, with rehearsed casual pauses and the delicacy of proper finger pressure—sudden and strong with a single note, gentle with the next. Subtle nuances that go undetected by the untrained eye and ear, making it look easy after hours upon hours of practice and sacrifice.

I get my first ovation in my new city, my new home. A standing ovation because I occupy the only piece of furniture in the tiny room. I peer through a bay window overlooking the street. A man walking a dog looks up and smiles at me. Anne takes my hand and leads me downstairs to see my private basement flat. We descend a wooden staircase, the railing smooth to the touch, as if recently refurbished.

I enter into pleasantness—a bed covered in a diamond-patterned quilt, a long dresser taking up half a wall, a standing mirror taller than me, and my own bathroom. I'm emotional again, but this time Anne holds me and says, "It's all right. You go be you. That's all you have to be." She points out a few things around the flat, then leaves me to familiarize myself with my new surroundings.

Later that night, after dinner, Matty and I take a stroll around Potrero Hill. Walking up and down steep hills is much different than traipsing around the flat desert. Shivering, I soon realize San Francisco is a different kind of cold compared to New Mexico's high-elevation cold. We stop at a small café and Matty buys me my first ever cappuccino. I feel special.

Sitting at a table for two as soft jazz plays in the background, Matty explains that he's a detective with the SFPD, and that if I ever find myself in trouble to just give him a call. He removes a new cell phone from his coat pocket and hands it to me, saying, "This is yours. My number and your auntie's number are already programmed in. You have to be careful around here."

"You have to be careful everywhere," I reply.

"True, true. But you're new in town, and some people sense that. Especially folks on the con. So, don't take shit from anyone and call me if some knucklehead gets out of line. You are free to do whatever you want around here and nobody's gonna suffocate you. Just be smart. I know you didn't fall off the turnip truck yesterday, but hey, if you need some help, call your cuz. All right?"

"No problem and thank you so much. Thanks for everything."

"Anytime. I'm here to protect and serve and to kick ass if

someone fucks with my family."

I give him a serious look and say, "You remind me of my mama. She don't take no crap from no one, but she's sly about it."

"Sly is good. Sly is smart," replies Matty. "Let's take a walk around The Hill. I'll show you a few places."

Off we go. Family taking care of family.

John Marshall traveled the world: Europe, Asia, South America. He wasn't the best-known jazzman, but he was one of the best paid and he made sure to take care of a trusted few and a few more after that: family, friends, fellow jazzmen and jazzwomen, an occasional hustler, an occasional politician.

My folks met while he was on tour in the southwest. He loved her, she loved him, and together they had me. John Marshall was a traveling jazzman, and my mama never thought he was anything other than that. I figure that's why their relationship worked. She knew what he was, he knew what she was, and neither one tried to be anything other than what they were. They both understood that trying to change another person was useless, unfair, and a waste of time.

My daddy was a great teacher of the piano. He also knew a thing or two about money, both making it and keeping it. I was his main music student, and we spent long hours together the few times I saw him each year. When together, it was just me, him, and a piano. By the time I was six, he'd set me up with the best classical piano instructor in Albuquerque. My Auntie Anne was his main student when it came to money, business dealings, and investment matters.

My daddy told me, "If you want to play the piano for a living, you have to practice and you have to play live. And when I say practice, I mean practice. It would also be wise to know the great jazz tunes and some classical music as well, even some popular tunes, but not too many of those. Don't spend more money than you've got, save ten percent of everything you make, and buy real estate for the long haul."

He set both of us up with knowledge and fundamentals. We reciprocated with eagerness and drive. "Take care of the people that matter. Take care of those in need—anyone hurting for money or food. You'll know if you can trust most people, and if they disappoint you, then only let them burn you once and learn from that hot flame."

His basic teachings made sense. All we had to do was heed sound advice in the ebb and flow of this thing called life.

What person in our lives—dead or alive—when their name is mentioned brings about an instant smile? John Marshall, my daddy, was that type of man.

TEN

JACK

There's a twinge in my stomach as the elevator descends. Contemplating the upcoming meeting induces an internal uneasiness. The smell of cleaning agents doesn't help. Destination: *The City Wrap* offices.

Rosenbaum and Smith await me as I enter the main conference room. The usual person sitting in there has business to discuss—a Silicon Valley executive, a banker, a building tenant, or a current or future vendor. Today it's just me, Rosenbaum, and Smith.

"Morning, Jack. Could you please shut the door?" are the first words out of Rosenbaum's mouth. The serious tone, combined with Smith's presence, causes me to take a mental step back, self-directing to a more attentive state as I close the door behind me.

The hopeful aroma of coffee is nonexistent, as I spy the unplugged coffeemaker on a corner counter. Unfortunately, there's no shortage of cheap aftershave drifting through the room.

"What's up, gentlemen?"

"Want to discuss Smith's article with you, the one that'll be running on the front page of the paper this week," replies Rosenbaum, still serious in tone.

"By the look of you two and the intense feeling in this room, I'm guessing the shit's about to hit the fan." I sit down at the conference table next to Smith, directly across from my mentor.

Not wasting time, Smith pipes in with, "I've dug up additional dirt on your uncle that connects him to Steve Jones in a bust a few years back."

"Bust?"

Smith looks at Rosenbaum, rotates his swivel chair so he's directly facing me, and says, "Pharmaceutical dope: painkillers, anti-anxiety pills, ED pills. Also, underage prostitution and child pornography."

I look at Smith, then tilt my head and look at Rosenbaum, before saying, "I thought Jones' main deal was armed robbery. By the way, what are ED pills?"

Rosenbaum joins in, saying, "You are partially correct. He was never arrested for anything other than armed robbery and assault. But he was present at this warehouse out in the Mission eleven years ago during a drug/porn/prostitution raid. He's listed in the police report but was never officially arrested."

Rosy, dropping the seriousness, almost laughs as he says, "On a side note, ED, my young friend, stands for erectile dysfunction. Boner pills. Something you don't have to worry about at your tender age."

Serious again, he continues. "So, who do you think the mysterious lieutenant with the SFPD was who oversaw the entire investigation and subsequent arrests, the one who handled the case from start to finish?"

"My uncle."

"Bingo," Smith says.

Rosenbaum pushes a transcription of the upcoming story across the table and says, "Because of your unexpected run-in with your uncle, I'm going to let you see what's coming down the pike. That's a rough copy. It's pretty close to what we're going to run with. Don't take it out of the building. Read it upstairs when you have some uninterrupted alone time. When you're done, get it back to me ASAP." He pauses until I nod. "The details are incontrovertible. Just so you know, we take several justified shots at your uncle, as well as at your buddy, Matthew."

I pick it up and give it a onceover. Rosenbaum goes on. "But what I'm about to say is more important than the article. Please hear me out on this, Jack. We think your uncle sent Jones out to do the robbery. We also think he sent Matty out to spy on you. I think he wanted to send you a message, which he did, and we think he wanted Jones dead, which, as you know, transpired."

He pauses and studies my best poker face. Satisfied I have nothing to say, he leans forward—elbows on the smooth table. "I doubt Matty knew anything about the Jones' connection with your uncle or that he was a hired gun. Your uncle rolled the dice on Matty reacting like a trained killer protecting a friend—you—and that he'd take out Jones if need be. Of course, we don't know for sure that Matty wasn't in on it." Rosy shakes his head as if embarrassed about telling a bad joke. Finally, he says, "I'm not sure if your uncle is a genius or just a crazy son of a bitch who planned a successful murder-send-a-message caper. On top of all that, he eliminated ties to a career criminal, one who can no longer offer a conflicting story because he's dead. Now, when he runs for mayor, it's his word against a corpse without a voice." Exhaling deeply, Rosy folds his hands around his belly and sits back in his chair.

I rub dry eyes and place my forehead on the conference table, saying, "Wow. I think I need a stiff drink and some depressing music." Suddenly fidgety, I lift my head and start drumming the table with my fingers. "This is serious stuff. You guys aren't fucking with me?"

Smith says, "I can speak for myself when I say this is some serious shit, my bartending friend. I'm also guessing you need to speak to Rosy here in private."

Smith gets up and heads for the door. Just prior to closing the conference room door, he turns and says, "Your uncle wouldn't have pulled this stunt for shits and giggles."

Not in the mood to engage, I keep my mouth shut while turning my head in Smith's direction. A blank stare is all he gets from me.

Smith gives zero fucks about my silence or my stare. "If I were you, Jack, I'd tell Rosy exactly what the hell you're hiding. I haven't been an investigative reporter in this town for this many years to suddenly lose my sense of smell. Especially when that something reeks of shit." With that, he gives me an odd look just before leaving, the door closing in his wake.

I face Rosy again. "Can I come over to your place tonight after I give the article a thorough read?" I add, "My uncle's seriously thinking about running for mayor?"

"Ten tonight. My place. Bring some of that scotch," is his answer to my first question. To my second question, he says, "Yes, he's been planning to make a run for mayor for some time. Or he thought he was going to run. I have no clue what that nutty bastard is going to do once this story breaks. But I can tell you this; he's not going to be happy about it. And that, Jack, is the understatement of the century. That's why the unprecedented sneak peek at tomorrow's news."

I stand up, draft in hand, and walk out of the conference room toward the elevators. Meeting adjourned.

I met him while attending San Francisco City College: Joseph Rosenbaum, the professor, my business instructor. He got my attention from the jump. Probably because he was already a successful businessman with a proven track record. He was not the typical professor who speaks only from a platform of theory.

Halfway through my final year of college I approach him with what I think is a solid business plan, including funding to back it up. My grand plan is to open a club using a large portion of the life insurance money I received after my father's death, a benefit which kicked in on my eighteenth birthday. I even have my mother's blessing if the professor thinks my plan has a chance at success.

He likes my plan so much that he wants in on the deal. He knows of an empty building situated off an alley not far from Market Street, one of the busiest streets in San Francisco. We can get space on the cheap, he tells me; a city lease tied to city wants, plus a low-interest loan and a long-term commitment. We have several meetings before agreeing on terms and launching our plan, with forty-nine percent ownership going to him and fifty-one percent to me. The topper is I won't have to use any of my own money and I'll have someone else sharing the burden—an experienced, successful businessman.

I run the show, do the heavy lifting, and have a wise, loyal advisor as my neighbor because Rosenbaum offers me the opportunity to move into what amounts to the attic at the top of *The City Wrap* building. I'm given a budget to remodel the storage area that sets across the lobby from Rosenbaum's penthouse suite. I consider it a gift for completing our bar project on time and under budget. In addition, I convince Rosenbaum to redirect his thinking regarding the billboard space perched atop the building. He bites, relinquishing control of the advertisement space. Without delay, I sway a young, aggressive Silicon Valley exec to commit to an all-inclusive deal showing off his company's new and shiny gadgets for the entire world to see when frequenting the busy touristy location.

Rosy's and my relationship is set in stone—business and otherwise.

ELEVEN

JACK

The Hall is closed on Mondays, which, on occasion, makes it my day off. After dropping Smith's transcript at my apartment, I descend downstairs and out into the city streets, making my way over to the club. I unlock the front door and silence the alarm, the hair on the back of my neck standing on end.

Too soon to feel comfortable.

I take it slow, swiveling my head as I look around. For what? Monsters, I guess. I grab what I need from the safe, prepare a large cup of cold brew to go, reset the alarm, lock the front door, and cruise toward the water.

Once on Market Street, I pick up my pace, speed-walking straight for the Ferry Building—darting around oblivious corporate types fingering handheld devices. I arrive to strong, swirling winds that muss my hair. I take a seat on an exposed bench facing the bay, looking out across the choppy water and up into the Oakland hills. I down most of the coffee and zip my coat up all the way. It feels good to be in the elements, my senses heightened.

A loud screech diverts my attention. A bold seagull lands on a nearby railing, looking for a handout. It's seen better days; a dull-gray dirty bird missing clumps of feathers. I doubt that my cold brew will satisfy its appetite. The only treasure I have rests on my lap in a sealed manila envelope. I look at it, lightly running a hand over the buff-colored paper. I'm not in a hurry. The seagull has no patience for me and flies away. *Better find a gullible tourist*, I think.

I open the envelope and remove its valuable contents, remembering where I was the first time I read it over ten years ago. There's a rapid-fire pounding in my ears—my heartbeat intensifying—as I begin to read. I wade through each paragraph, feeling his pain anew. Raw. Disturbing. My anger fresh, I reach his final statement.

A piece of me was stolen and I can't get it back. Sorry, but I have to do what I have to do. I love you. Goodbye.

It's time to make a play and share Sean's letter with Rosenbaum. I laugh in a way that defines the moment, thinking, *I can't believe this shit is happening to me*, although I sensed all along that the letter would someday find its way back into my life. That day has come.

I place the letter inside the envelope and hunker into the weathered bench, my backside pressing into soft, moist wood. I drink what's left of my coffee while looking out at the wind-whipped bay—whitecaps pushing across murky water—and catch a whiff of garlicy butter coming from who knows where. All of a sudden I'm hungry.

I'm ready to head home to grab a bite to eat, do some reading before attending a nighttime meeting. A letter and a bottle of Laphroaig will be in hand when I knock on the professor's door.

TWELVE

MATTY

As I step from the shadows in the parking lot at Ocean Beach, I startle the assistant chief's driver/ bodyguard/thug associate, Neil Stanza, also a cop, also a killer. Facing me, he keeps a predetermined distance. "Chief needs a few minutes to himself before you go down there," Stanza says.

Looking out toward the ocean, I see O'Shea's silhouette, along with a small ember glow. I go that way, ignoring Stanza's instructions, saying, "Fuck you, white boy." The burly veteran cop says nothing in return, knowing full well he's dealing with a fellow killer. The back of my skull tingles, knowing he's staring daggers at me.

I make my approach, wading through pungent smoke wafting through the air. "Didn't Stanza tell you to give me a little more time?" O'Shea asks, his back to me.

I trudge through five more feet of sand. "That cracker didn't say shit to me. I don't think he likes my kind."

He turns and faces me, adjusting his pants. "I doubt he ignored a direct order, but I think you're right when you say he doesn't like your kind."

Getting right to the point, I ask, "What do you want, David?"

"You don't work for me as of right now. You're being transferred to the academy for a three-month stint. Instructor's position. After ninety days, when things cool down a bit, you'll be promoted to lieutenant and transferred somewhere other than vice."

"I guess it's time for us to go our separate ways," I reply.

"It is that time. There's going to be some lies dispensed in that paper. Nothing I can't handle. The Jew is going to run a story that makes me look bad, makes you look bad as well. But I'll catch the heat and they'll forget about you in no time. I'm the one they want to disgrace. Any questions?"

"None."

"Good. One last thing. I know you have ties with my nephew, or you used to. I'd hate to see a quote in that paper attached to your name."

"Last time I looked in the mirror I didn't see a dumb motherfucker. Jack and I go back a few years, but what took place between you and me stays between me and you. And, as far as I know, everything between us was on the up and up, unless—right this second—you're telling me otherwise."

We exchange even, steady glares, then I say, "Everything's cool between us. Just like it's always been."

O'Shea, mulling things over, takes a hit on the fat cigar before slowly blowing out smoke and saying, "As you say, 'everything is cool between us.' You're dismissed."

I turn around and see Stanza standing where the parking lot pavement meets sandy beach. I head his way. Stanza's gun is drawn, held at his side, the dark metallic extension barely visible. I let fly a high-pitched whistle. A modified car's engine comes to life at the far end of the parking lot, a mid-sixties Impala—long, menacing, gray in color with purple undertones looking like sharkskin under the bright lights of the parking lot. It slowly rolls toward Stanza, windows down.

A brief hint of surprise comes and goes on the bodyguard's face as he turns toward the vehicle motoring his way. The three hardcore brothers sitting inside make sure he sees they're heavily armed. Caught off guard, Stanza doesn't know what to do. The car stops within ten feet of him. Stanza can clearly see the driver, as I do. The guy is wearing dark sunglasses and a ski cap. He returns Stanza's stare. The two men in the back seat keep shotguns at the ready.

I quickly approach Stanza. Brushing his right shoulder with that of my left, I take the gun from his hand and say, "You're not that smart, cracker." Walking up to the Impala, I open the front passenger door and get inside. The barrel of the nearest shotgun eases out an open window, pointing directly at Stanza's center mass. He doesn't move, doesn't even blink.

Slanting my head out the window, I utter my final remarks before the car drives away. "Thanks for the gun. You can go wipe your ass now, white-bread."

I'm driven home by the men who came to pick me up, fellow cops and committed associates. It's time for me to be cunning and smart and fearless. Hopefully, more cunning and smart and fearless than my former boss.

I paid attention to my uncle's stoic teachings. I'm also a jazzman. But my instruments just happen to be a brain, a gun, and balls the size of Texas grapefruits.

58

THIRTEEN

JACK

Crossing the lobby, I knock on Rosenbaum's door. "Come in," is the gruff response from the other side. I turn the handle and enter, carrying an envelope, Smith's article, and a dark green bottle of scotch.

Rosenbaum, placing ice cubes in tumblers, looks up and says, "Take it into the front room. Let's do this in comfort." Reversing course, I narrow in on a deep-cushioned leather chair. I sit opposite its twin; a teak coffee table separating the two.

Rosenbaum sets the tumblers on coasters and I fill them halfway. We grip weighty crystal and clink glasses. Rosenbaum settles in, takes a sip of whiskey, and asks, "What did you think of Smith's piece?"

"Detailed, thorough, somewhat surprising." I take a double sip before continuing. "How did he get access to all that information?"

"As you can imagine, your uncle has mostly enemies within the police department. I doubt you're surprised. Also, Smith has sources within the department—as well as outside the department—with close ties to the well-connected. I don't know who they are and don't ask. He would never tell, nor should he." Rosy stops talking and savors the booze, taking a lengthy pull. "That man is by far the best reporter I've ever been associated with. Once he sniffs something out, he's relentless about getting to the bottom of things. He's the real deal when it comes to investigative journalism."

"The dude does seem intense."

Disregarding my comment, Rosenbaum continues. "Let me tell you a story about Smith. He was a new reporter, young, just graduated from USF and gets hired at *The Wrap*. His first real writing job. This was in the early seventies. He's green, so he's assigned bullshit, new-guy-reporter grunt work. Right out of the chute he writes this story, on his own time by the way, detailing steroid abuse related to top-tier athletes. Basically, Olympic athletes and professional athletes.

"Back then, most people assumed that strength athletes, such as weightlifters and bodybuilders, were the only athletes taking what they called 'the juice.' Those supposedly in the know blithered that if it extended beyond the strength disciplines it would mostly be found in Eastern and Central Europe. Not in North America. Certainly not in the good ole USA. That was bullshit then and it's bullshit today.

"By the late sixties, and especially around the '72 Olympics and thereafter, performance enhancing drugs, or PEDs as they're called today, were being distributed worldwide. Most top-tier athletes will put anything into their bodies if they think it will give them even the slightest competitive edge."

"Athletes back in the day were on the juice?"

"Not all of them. I would say a high percentage, though. The mainstream media, the owners of major league sports teams, and most athletes all looked the other way. They conveniently played dumb. Or denied that PEDs existed within their specific sport. The article was an eyeopener for those who chose to read it and give it credence. It was well-written, well-sourced, well-researched."

Rosy pauses to savor more whiskey. Appearing satisfied, he continues where he left off. "Nobody of significance in the sports world took Smith's article seriously. So when the baseball steroid era finally began making news around the country, along with doping scandals connected to top-tier cyclists, swimmers, and track athletes across the globe, Smith forwarded copies of his original article, along with his research notes, to the commissioners of the major professional and amateur sports organizations in both this country and abroad. He even sent a copy to the talking heads at ESPN." He takes another sip, then an angered tone creeps in, "But if it's not on a teleprompter, they don't speak to it. At least not out loud for the world to hear."

Rosy swirls the brown liquid before downing what's left. Placing elbows on knees and leaning forward, he's ready to conclude his tale. "The story was completely ignored. 'Heads in the sand,' as Smith would say. Jack, my boy, that man might be a dinosaur but he's always been a step ahead of his peers." Done with touting Smith's talents, he looks at the manila envelope resting on the arm of the chair I occupy. His eyes go from the envelope, to me, then back to the envelope.

I tap the envelope and say, "This is what Smith was alluding to. My uncle wants what's inside or wants it to go away. I figure once he decided to enter into politics, he couldn't risk guessing whether it existed or not. But if it did exist, and obviously it does, I'd be the only person on the planet in possession of it. I've had this letter for over ten years and haven't read it in that long either," I stop as memories flood in, then finish, "until this morning, when I removed it from the safe at The Hall."

"What's in the letter?"

I hand him the envelope containing Sean's letter, and say, "It's my cousin's suicide note. My Uncle David's son's suicide letter."

Rosenbaum removes the letter from the envelope and reads it silently. I look into my glass before gulping it down to melting cubes. Rosenbaum gives the letter a second read. When done, he looks up and says, "Holy shit, Jack. You've kept this to yourself all these years? This is some damning stuff. Even if your uncle denied doing these things, public opinion would eat him alive. No wonder he decided to send you a message. Has he ever flat-out asked you if his son left this for you?"

"He kind of grilled me the day Sean died, definitely asking if Sean left me a note. But at the time, I had no idea the suicide letter existed. I'd just found out Sean was dead. As I broke down, he could tell I was receiving that terrible news for the first time. In the back of my mind, though—and maybe his, too—I figured Sean would leave me some clue as to what went wrong and what caused him to do what he did. After I left my uncle's house the night of Sean's death, I went straight home. Straight to the attic above our garage. Sean would sometimes leave me things in a box that I kept up there. Lo and behold, there it was. I took it down to Ocean Beach and read it. At first, it shocked me. But after reading it a few times, it all made sense. I believe every word."

We sit in silence for a minute or two. Finally, Rosenbaum says, "What do you want to do? I mean, if you want, I'll hold onto it. Put it in a safe place. I can easily do that and not share it with anyone. It'll stay between us. Any copies?"

"No, just the original. I don't know what I want to do with it, Professor. Maybe nothing. You hold onto it. Let's figure this out together. But first, could you do me a favor?"

"Name it."

"Let Smith read it. Correct me if I'm wrong, but he needs to know what's at stake here."

"I think you're right." He fidgets with his lower lip, pinching it between right thumb and index finger, before saying, "I take that back. I know you're right. Okay, we'll let Smith read the letter, digest it, understand what he's up against. After that, it goes into the safest of safe places. Don't worry—absolutely no one will have access to it but me. And if I should get hit by a Muni bus, it will miraculously find its way back to you."

"What happens if that same bus takes me out?"

"Then Smith will end up with it," replies Rosenbaum, as he adds, "You did right by sharing it with me, with another human being. It must've been tough holding onto such a brutal secret all this time. Man, Jack, I'm so sorry."

More scotch is consumed. More strategic planning is bantered about. More ideas are kicked around, however ridiculous they seem. A phone call is made to Smith, with a meeting confirmed for the following day.

Finally, Rosy gives me a bearhug before I leave. No article in hand. No letter in hand. No bottle in hand because the bottle is empty.

I stumble into my flat, listing to the left and hoping for a soft landing in the bathroom. I don't make it that far. Spin, spin, spin goes the king-size bed, as I stare at the ceiling, blinking, swallowing, unable to stop the whirl.

FOURTEEN

JASMINE

I wake early with a slight tightness in my stomach, a tension brought on by nerves and excitement. A normal feeling I actually enjoy. It's supposed to be there; if not, something's wrong. Since childhood, that feeling always surfaces before a gig. The audition at The Hall will be no different.

Preparation revolves around a tight time frame. But that doesn't matter because I pour myself into practicing whenever—midday, late night, early morning—while ignoring the need for sleep. That will come later. I grin when Matty says, "You'll own that place on Sundays. It'll be your special place, same as what your pops had out in the Fillmore at a club called Mo's."

Matty gives me the rundown on Jack. Their rekindled friendship. How they met way back when. Jack being a standup guy. And a bunch of other useless information thrown in for good measure. He also includes his take on the club manager, Ana. Even though he doesn't know her that well, she's left a lasting impression. Finally, he rattles off a half dozen high-level acts that have played on the same stage I'm about to audition on.

I'm more than ready. A couple of years in the city has given me time to meet other people, especially at church. Friends I met early on will deliver my recently purchased August Hoffman baby grand piano, a discontinued 2008 model constructed in China with German hammers and strings and a solid spruce soundboard. It was refurbished by a piano company on the East Coast, just outside D.C., and sold at a bargain price, a little under seven grand, which couldn't be passed up. My church, Glow Memorial, purchased the piano for me as a gift for services rendered. I'm crushed by the kindness of the parents of the underprivileged children I've taught. Those who have so little to give seem to always give more.

I've performed with other local musicians at several small venues sprinkled throughout the city. But The Hall offers opportunity—an opportunity to land a solo gig. Just me, with minor accompaniment and a polished baby grand. If landed, it won't be a good paying gig. But that's not the point. It could turn into a regular, consistent gig, and that *is* the point. A place to earn a reputation. A place to be seen and heard. This could be my opportunity come knocking and I want to excel.

Jack told Matty he'd give me a solid thirty minutes to play whatever I want to play. No rules. No restrictions. My audition. I'll play a variety of musical selections, from classical, to jazz, to contemporary. In total, six pieces, with vocals on two of the numbers—cover tunes by Nora Jones and Bruce Hornsby. Whether Jack likes me or not, the folks attending the audition are going to see a skilled, well-rehearsed musician. The pastel blue dress picked out by Auntie Anne is pressed and ready.

When audition day arrives, my cohorts, fellow musicians

Coby Baller and Cameron Oliver, arrive early in a heavy-duty delivery truck. Sitting in Matty's car, parked no more than twenty yards away, I watch as they're greeted in a side alley leading up to a roll-up door. They're met by a woman I don't recognize. Matty pipes in, "That's Ana." Strapped to a piano dolly, the baby grand is lowered via hydraulic lift until it rests on solid ground. The smooth transition from outside to inside takes but a few minutes.

This won't be my first time at Jack's club. I've been there once before to have drinks with friends. I remember the stage as an elevated fixture that's impossible to miss, a dominant angled platform at the back of the club. There are also denim sound panels installed off the bar's open ceiling to allow for better sound transfer and decibel control. With a concrete floor, I'm sure they were a must or shouting back and forth would be the only way to communicate.

Coby and Cameron will also set up two small amplifiers, one for my microphone, the other for the bass guitar. Lastly, a bare-bones drum set will be assembled—snare, tom-tom, bass, cymbals. I'll have accompaniment on songs with vocals.

Time to go inside. Flutter, flutter goes my stomach.

"Go knock 'em dead," says Matty.

FIFTEEN

JACK

Matty and Jasmine show up a few minutes early, all eyes immediately shifting to the beautiful pianist with braided brown hair and sharp green eyes. She's wearing a calf-length wool coat that conceals what's underneath. Matty handles introductions. When he gets to me, well, I'm a bit tongue-tied, floored by Jasmine's natural beauty. While I'm searching for words, out from the kitchen comes Mike Gates, parking himself on a barstool and nodding in Jasmine's direction. She acknowledges the chef with a return nod, then looks at me and asks, "Is it okay if I begin?"

After an awkward pause on my part, Ana quickly chimes in, saying, "Certainly," before looking at me like I need to get a grip.

I finally gain verbal footing, overcompensating with multiple responses, "Absolutely. Please begin. Yes, of course. Whenever you'd like to start. Please do."

Removing her coat and handing it to Matty, the lean, sensuous musician floats toward the stage in a simple yet elegant blue dress. Her performance attire accentuates the color of her smooth, bronze skin, as well as draping a fine silhouette. Everyone continues to watch as she walks up the far ramp. Once on stage, she hugs her fellow musicians. Finally, she glides over to the polished wooden bench and takes a seat at the piano.

I'm overwhelmed by Jasmine's presence and stunned by the resemblance and similarity of her skin's hue and tone—a close match to that of my deceased cousin. She's beyond gorgeous yet appears unassuming.

Jasmine sits at the piano—favoring the front third of the bench—and slowly lifts the fallboard and positions her hands ever so lightly on the keys. She takes in a deep breath, her chest expanding, before letting it out bit by bit. She begins with a piece by Mozart. It doesn't take long before those in attendance shed tears as sights and sounds strike emotional chords. Her playing looks effortless, smooth, producing a sound that emanates grace and elegance. From Mozart to Thelonious Monk, she goes through the audition cycle, everyone in the palm of her hands as she transitions from Monk to Duke Ellington, from Ellington to Wynton Marsalis.

Jasmine saves the songs with vocals for last. The other two musicians are ready, motivated by her playing. Of all the numbers, the final two are straightforward arrangements, allowing the musicians freedom to take off and fly, worry-free from musical mishap. They ease into it. Jasmine's voice is clean and smooth with, at times, a hint of throatiness.

After completing the fifth song, Jasmine pauses to take a sip of water. The audience looks on, hooked, mesmerized, ready to be fed. We're listening to a classically trained pianist with jazz-infused blood. Jasmine looks at her bandmates, giving them a visual nudge that asks, "You ready?" The answer to her question is, "Hell yeah!", as they jump into *The Way It Is* by Bruce Hornsby and the Range.

The number opens with piano only. After a smooth bass line, the drums kick in. They're off and running, from a slow intro to a steady ride, to total synchronicity: *That's just the way it is. But don't you believe it.* Through the middle of the song all three musicians are flying, jamming, building and building: *That's just the way it is. Some things will never change.* They roar toward crescendo, reaching for eventual climax. Finally, the descent, as they trail off, off, off, until silence. Total silence.

Mike Gates is the first to leap to his feet and shout appreciation, beginning what amounts to a standing ovation from all in attendance—by happenstance or not. Jasmine and the band are ear-to-ear smiles as they drink from their respective water bottles and acknowledge each other with nods and facial smirks: musician validation. Jasmine looks over at me. Just a look. After two heartbeats, I say, "You got the gig." Jasmine leaps from the bench and throws herself at her fellow musicians. There are hugs all around before the rest of us travel up to the stage.

Mike Gates shouts, "I cook for everyone. We must celebrate. Who trained you in the classical?"

Jasmine looks at the chef as he walks down the ramp toward the kitchen. She speaks to his back, "My classical teacher in Albuquerque is Lithuanian."

"Of course, teacher is Lithuanian," shouts the happy man.

I look at Jasmine and say, "Why don't you and Ana talk particulars regarding when you can start playing here regularly." Jasmine and Ana head down the ramp and over to the bar as the other two musicians break down and house their respective instruments.

Once everybody settles in at the bar, Mike Gates hustles

out plate after plate of food for the hungry musicians. Ana and Jasmine agree to an early afternoon schedule from twelve-thirty to four for twelve consecutive Sundays. Jasmine will play three one-hour sets, with two fifteen-minute breaks in between. Every Sunday she'll honor her church choir commitment and then make her way downtown for her gig at The Hall. Cold brew and Lousy Lime Water flow as the early morning drinking crowd watches the celebration wind down at the far end of the bar.

Ana and I inform Jasmine that we always take out a series of advertisements in *The Daily Wrap* to hype new performers. I ask her to give me a call the following day so we can schedule a not-so-distant appointment with the ad crew over at *The Wrap.*

Jasmine asks, "Do you think that's necessary? I don't want to put you out or anything."

"Yeah, I do think it's necessary. We need to get the word out."

Ana and I sport happy faces as we hand over business cards to Jasmine. Goodbyes are said, and the musicians and detective drift from The Hall.

With another day's business well underway, Ana punches me in the arm and says, "Someone was smitten by the charm of a certain musician."

"I think everyone who witnessed that performance was smitten with the charm of that lovely lady. Please correct me if I'm wrong."

"No correction needed. You're a thousand percent right. But don't tell me you weren't taken aback by Jasmine. And I'm not talking about her performance."

"I can't deny that either." We both laugh before turning and going our separate ways.

As I enter the kitchen, Mike Gates announces, "This is special thing what is happening today. Sunday will be big day forward going. You watch, boss. Big things I feel." He grunts and gives me a crooked grin before heading for the alley to smoke an unfiltered cigarette.

74

SIXTEEN

JACK

The stacked, front-page headline on the first-off-the-press copies reads:

Smith's article in *The City Wrap* is detailed and revealing. Little is held back regarding David O'Shea's tainted career. The only thing not uncovered—and truly the most damning piece of information that could be used against the assistant chief—is the suicide letter left behind by his son. Certain members of the police force, as well as a scattering of loyal followers, will now be forced to take a defensive posture. I'm betting it all on my uncle being one pissed off hombre.

Rosenbaum and a trusted few gather at *The City Wrap* offices. The topic of the evening's discussion: repercussions from the powerful and angry. *Be prepared for anything imaginable* is the recycled mantra.

Unable to shed worry, I try to convince Allen Smith to get a bodyguard. Smith pooh-poohs my suggestion, saying, "I've come this far on my own. If your uncle hires someone to kill me, well, so be it. It's not a macho thing, it's a just-the-way-I-am thing. But thanks anyway, Jack." I feel downright ridiculous offering advice to a grown man. I'm also a little embarrassed about being politely shot down by the seasoned beat writer, but I'm happier than not for making the effort.

Earlier, I asked Matty for a favor: "Could you please keep an eye on The Hall every now and then when you're in that part of town?"

Matty's response: "No problem, especially since I have family working there. Don't worry, I got your back." He correctly gauged my predicament, which makes me glad I decided to trust him. I overdid my thank yous, which made him a bit uncomfortable, but he understood because he's the kind of guy who understands the power of fear.

"Business as usual," shouts Rosenbaum, as the meeting breaks up and everyone files out of the conference room. "We will deal with whatever comes our way when it comes our way. Call me if you need anything. And remember, my lawyer is at the ready twenty-four seven."

I take the short elevator ride up to my apartment, knowing full well sleep might not come, that the scary thinking circling my brain might linger for a while. I'm right on both accounts.

I can imagine my uncle reading the front-page headline. *Fuck me,* his likely response. I'm sure his minions will be at his beck and call, all at a heightened sense of career survival as they do as they're told. Not one of them balking at orders given. Play-acting as if everyone is on the same page.

At some point he'll have to deal with his bosses: the chief and the mayor, neither of whom are on his Christmas card list. Predictable as it seems, deny, deny, deny will be his partial defense strategy regarding Smith's scathing article. Coincidence; bizarre circumstance; wrong place, wrong time; and bullshit journalism will round out the remainder of his argument. The mayor and the chief, both non-supporters of David O'Shea, will temporarily commit to supporting him, the illusion of a united front within the ranks of the police department and City Hall. I wonder how long that will last.

The first sign of attack happens hours after the controversial issue of *The City Wrap* hits the streets. Immigration officials show up at The Hall to hassle Mike Gates. I guess my uncle can't let my relationship with Rosenbaum go. He must view it as an *us against him* thing. I make the required call. At first, Rosy tolerates my whining, as I carry on about *guilt by association* and the *unfairness of it all.* At his wit's end with my bitching, he interrupts and says he's hanging up to call his attorney, Michelle Vieira. Rosy lives in a world where problems, no matter their size, have solutions.

After receiving her marching orders from my agitated business partner, Vieira makes her way over to The Hall, pronto, to shoo away the federal employees. Once done escorting them from the building, she loudly expresses her non-humble, lawyerly opinion: "Those jackoffs don't have a pot to piss in." Mike Gates has no clue as to pots and pissing but is relieved when "the communist fucks" are made to leave.

At Rosy's insistence, Vieira passes along the two officials' names to Allen Smith, who contacts trusted sources within the immigration department. He determines who the lackeys work for and ties their immediate supervisor into an acquaintanceship with the assistant chief—a recent online photo of the pair gripping and grinning at a fundraiser. I'm not surprised. Smith will more than likely use that information against my uncle in a follow-up story.

Smith knows the powerful usually deny damaging allegations and sidestep accurate journalism as if it's society's oozing sore. However, Smith also knows that a large percentage of *The City Wrap's* dedicated readers, a savvy bunch, are not allied with the assistant chief. They're smart enough to know when smoke is being blown up their asses. A lie is a lie, and the truth is the truth.

The second sign of attack is when an employee from the labor board shows up at The Hall to ascertain if an underage girl is working there. I view Isabella's time spent at the bar as an internship, an internship compensated for by an under-the-table fair and equitable wage. Also, it's private . . . between me and Isabella and Ana. It's no one else's business. Vieira, still there, takes care of the issue as she listens to a repeated lecture on violating a juvenile's rights from an uninformed and over-matched Labor Board stooge. Vieira shows the over-eager knucklehead the door, barely holding back a barrage of profanity, but dropping several unpleasant wisecracks disguised as polite *fuck yous*. The lady lawyer has quite a mouth on her.

Upset at my uncle, because who else could be orchestrating this bullshit, I call Rosenbaum again. I'm not done venting. I barely utter *hello* before Rosy beats me to the punch, telling me about a package that mysteriously showed up at *The City Wrap* offices addressed to Smith. Even weirder, it was emitting a sound, not a ticking sound, but a humming, scratching sound.

The bomb squad was notified, and the package was carefully removed from the building by a robot before being X-rayed. Within the package was a fatally wounded wharf rat. The cops let Smith take several photos of the dead rat. Additional ammo for a future story.

The final straw is when Isabella is approached at school by a stranger who hands her a note. He appears in the hallway as she comes out of the restroom with a fellow student. Unbeknownst to him, the brave little girl pulls out her cell phone at the last second and snaps a quick profile pic as he walks away. She texts me and Ana, giving us a brief summary regarding the unidentified man—dressed in all-black and a hat and sunglasses—before hightailing it back to class.

SEVENTEEN

JACK

We race over to the school in a panic. The note consists of three words: WATCH YOUR BACK. It's official . . . an obvious warning has been issued.

School administrators are apologetic and frantic at the same time, embarrassed that a total stranger walked onto their campus and made contact with a student. I'm silently livid. Ana directs a series of F-bombs at those in charge, who wisely grin and bear it. Yet we're both relieved that Isabella is fine and taking it all in stride. We remove her from school, taking her back to The Hall.

I decide to do what any desperate man would do—I call a powerful, ballsy advocate. My mother.

"Hello."

"Ma, it's Jack."

"How are you?"

"Have you read the paper today?"

"I have. Why?"

"The *Chronicle* or *The City Wrap*?"

"The *Chronicle*. You know I rarely read *The City Wrap*.

I've had a subscription to the *Chronicle* since before you were born."

"Do me a huge favor, Mom. Go get a copy of today's *City Wrap*. Read the feature story. You can't miss it. It's about Uncle David. After you've read it, give me a call and we'll talk."

"Okay, son. And, like I asked earlier, how are you?"

"I'm fine, but I have to go. Call me when you finish the article. I love you."

"Love you, too."

Ana overhears the entire conversation and raises her eyebrows as I hang up. I give her a determined look, and say, "My mom can put a stop to this crap. Uncle David will listen to her, at least for a little while."

"How do you know that'll work?" asks Ana.

"Because they have a long history and she's a tough Norwegian broad who takes absolutely no shit from anybody. If my mom and Allen Smith had a child, he or she would be the dictator of a small country. A compassionate dictator ruling with an iron fist who drinks too much tequila and makes delicious Krumcake cookies."

"I hope you're right."

"On this, I am right. You'll see."

Three hours later, I receive a call from my mom. She invites me over for dinner, refusing to take *no* for an answer. Also—in a few harsh words—she tells me that future, serious conversations with her will take place in person and not on the phone. I agree to her demand, apologize for rushing things, and let her know I'll see her at the house at seven on the dot.

EIGHTEEN

JACK

As I stroll up the driveway, a fresh bottle of cold brew in tow, it dawns on me that I haven't seen my mom in at least six months. We've had plenty of phone conversations, but zero face-to-face time. I walk in the front door and call out to her. "In here," is her response. I head for the kitchen.

"Look at you," she says, walking over to greet me with a hug and kiss on the cheek. "Someone looks a little thin. You need a woman to fatten you up," she says, as she returns to the stove to resume dinner prep.

"You're right about the woman part, Ma. But I don't need one for cooking."

"You're not unique when it comes to that, young man. How are you, truly?"

"I'm okay. A little stressed out over the obvious. Did you read the article?"

"I did. Your uncle seems to be up to no good if you believe that story, which I have no reason to doubt."

"Believe it. And he keeps on causing more problems like

the ones I told you about on the phone before you cut me off and forced me over here."

"Forced you. You're lucky I don't smack you for that comment."

"You know I'm kidding, Ma. I seriously need your help. He's messing with children. You've met Isabella."

"I have met that precious little girl. Now, let's sit down and eat. The food's ready. And then you can tell me what you need from me."

Once dinner is over, as I hover over dessert—warm pie and cold brew—I ask, "So you're okay with giving Uncle David a call and asking him to dial it down a notch?"

"I'll call him. However, I will word things properly so he can save face. You know he is a stubborn man. He doesn't like to be told what to do. I will ask him for a favor. I have not spoken to him or your aunt in quite a while. After your cousin died, things changed. I think that's probably normal. If I'm being honest, I never really felt comfortable around either one of them. But I will make the call. You can count on that."

"I appreciate what you're doing for me, Ma."

"You'd better appreciate me, young man. Now get going and make sure you find a woman before you're too old."

"Scandinavian?" I ask.

"You know that doesn't matter to me. Just find a nice woman. Hopefully, one who knows her way around the kitchen."

"I'll do my best. Love you, Ma. Goodnight."

Before returning downtown, I take a quick detour to what used to be my cousin's house. I feel like contemplating simpler times. Driving slowly, I catch the slightest movement from inside a parked car. Someone just sitting there. The car is parked halfway between my mom's house and Sean's old house, facing the opposite direction I'm driving. My take is that it's a woman. I log it into memory. Could be nothing. Feels like something. They're still there when I leave.

My uncle will soon chill out. For how long? Who knows? I've prompted a short-term fix. Odds-on it won't last. I feel like a dumbass for putting a Band-Aid on a bullet wound. A slight reprieve will give me time to think and, hopefully, time to arrive at a real solution. My world has gone batshit crazy and things won't get back to normal as long as certain monsters roam the city.

I have a new concern: my mother's safety.

I'm not surprised when he stops by to see his mother. Not unusual.

I am surprised he heads my way when leaving. He's going the wrong way. Sinking into the seat, I exhale as he passes, not knowing if he sees someone sitting alone in a car or not. Does it really matter?

I remain still, waiting as he parks in front of that house. What the hell is he doing? Fucking reminiscing?

Ten minutes later he leaves, this time driving by in the opposite direction. I look straight ahead, following with my eyes until he hangs a left at the end of the street. His head never tilts up toward the rearview mirror. Probably didn't notice a thing. Either way, time to scoot.

The ringtone surprises me early the following morning.

"Hello."

"Jack, it's your mother."

"I know. That's why I answered."

"Don't be a smartass."

"Too late."

"I spoke with your uncle last night. He agreed to look into the issues your employees recently experienced. However, he said your friends at the newspaper are none of his concern."

"Mom, did you call him at home or on his cell phone?

"I called the house, Jack. It's the only number I have."

"Who answered?

Nobody answered. I left a message on their machine; it's likely he was still at work. He called back a few hours later. Why do you ask?"

"Just wondering. Thanks for helping me out."

"You're welcome."

NINETEEN

JACK

The Hall is packed for Jasmine's first performance. Word has gotten out as friends, family, and huge support from San Francisco's church community leave not a single seat unoccupied. Standing room only onlookers spill onto what's left of vacant floor space.

Ana and I had estimated that three-hundred people would show for the first event. In reality, it looks like somewhere in the mid four-hundreds. Our employees are in full-on hustle mode in an attempt to keep up with thirsty, hungry guests. Ana whispers in my ear, "Could you imagine if we would've charged admission?"

"Wouldn't've been the right thing to do," I reply, before adding, "I can certainly do the math at ten bucks a head, though."

"Try doing the math at twenty bucks a head," she counters.

Jasmine meets Isabella, seems enamored with her, and asks that she take a seat at the piano for her first set. Nearer proximity will allow Isabella a better opportunity to feel the music, to touch and detect the reverb and amplification on stage.

Matty also meets Isabella, adapting to her disability and pushing to communicate like he's known her for years. Isabella shows the detective the pic of the man in black who approached her at school. Matty asks her to send him the image, mouthing the question slowly. She sends it over once they exchange cell numbers. He tells her if she ever needs help, if the cat in black shows up again, to call or text and he'll make her request a priority. They bump fists as Isabella takes Jasmine's hand, guiding her to the stage.

Matty leans toward me and says, "Beautiful little girl. Tough. Smart. Food for thought—I would have charged admission."

"So I've been told."

Ana, standing in front of a microphone, introduces Jasmine to the waiting audience.

Jasmine takes it from there, accompanied by Coby and Cameron, sticking with a sure thing. What lies ahead is a string of classical, pop, jazz, gospel and R&B tunes.

Old school jazz finishes the first one-hour set. A thunderous ovation fills the air as Jasmine leaves the stage, holding Isabella's hand. Ana escorts them into the backroom and over to the open roll-up door. Jasmine steps outside, breathing in city air, decompressing in a cooler environment. "Wow, the audience was amazing. Is it going to be like this every week?" Jasmine says.

"That's up to you," I reply, adding, "It'll probably thin out as time goes by. But I have a strong feeling you are one talented young lady in the midst of establishing a following. If a jam-packed house is a problem, it's a good one to have."

Matty pipes in. "Extremely good problem to have, Cuz."

Ana brings the outside crowd a round of water. The

atmosphere is light and happy and joyous. All of us—the band, me, Ana, Matty, and Isabella—can feel the good mojo in the air.

Fifteen minutes fly by as they saunter back in for their next set. The crowd hasn't thinned, it's grown.

Eight members from her church choir join Jasmine on stage. The next hour is filled with gospel songs. From slow to fast, from low to high, the choir sings with support from the band. Those in attendance are witnessing a well-rehearsed, top-notch act. Jasmine and company leave the stage for another break before jumping into the final set.

Outside in the alley, musicians hug and say their goodbyes. The final set will be a solo act. Before going back up on stage, Jasmine follows me into the kitchen. I stop and say, "You lost?"

"Not at all. I was wondering if we could grab dinner tonight?"

"Me and you?" I ask, surprised by the question.

"Just me and you."

"Sure. What time? Where do you want to go?"

"Your place. Cook something simple. Steaks. Maybe some red wine. I'll be there around seven. I know where you live."

"Done deal. See you at seven. Now, go break a leg."

TWENTY

JACK

As Jasmine leaves the kitchen, my mind races. I mentally earmark two steaks from the restaurant walk-in cooler, thankful I already have a decent bottle of red wine at home. Is the house clean? Bachelor clean . . . which means not good enough. I'll have to get home by five to dial it in. I also have to clean up: shower, shave, fresh clothes. I'm giddy. Beauty can do that to you.

She only plays three numbers during her final set, all classical. The shortest being fifteen minutes long. The majority of the crowd stays put, fixed in their seats. Maybe fifty people drift away between the second and third sets. Mike Gates, sitting at the bar, mouths *wow!* in my direction.

At last, Jasmine announces the final song, a number by Chopin. Off she goes. When done, it seems like those who took part in the entire performance are exhausted due to an unexpected emotional workout. The appreciative applause brings tears as she bows and thanks them all. After coming off stage, she sticks around, speaking with whoever wants a piece of her. Half an hour passes before complimentary exchanges dissipate. Not ready to make an exit, Jasmine retreats to the bar to hang out with Mike Gates. She sips chilled Russian vodka while he heralds her with wild stories about the Motherland.

At five, Ana, Isabella, and I get ready to leave. As I kiss Ana and Isabella goodbye, Ana says, "You seem awfully upbeat."

"Who wouldn't be, after today's packed house?"

"It's something more than that, mister. What's in the bag?"

"Well, I think I'll keep the 'something more than that' part to myself. What's in the bag is also none of your business," I say, shifting the sack I'm carrying behind my back.

"Be careful, my friend," is Ana's advice, as Isabella signs goodbye prior to mother and daughter walking away.

After unlocking the door, I hustle straight through the apartment and out the back door, taking the steps leading up to the roof two at a time. I remove the protective cover on the grill that's stationed on the concrete walkway. I prepare the coals, loading them into a neat, centered pile on the bottom grate before setting the coals afire with the help of a long match and lighter fluid.

Back inside, I jump headfirst into a cleaning frenzy, hiding all those things a man trying to make a good impression hides . . . like everyday man stuff. I check the freezer for vodka—relieved to find a nearly full bottle of Kettle One inside. Eyeballing the wine rack, I select a four-year-old bottle of Merlot. I wash wine glasses and tumblers, two each, before searching for matching plates, knives, forks, and spoons. Not an easy task.

With everything in its proper place, I take a quick shower and get dressed: jeans, laced boots, a pullover sweater. At seven on the nose, I place the steaks on the grill, uncork the wine, slam a shot of vodka, and dial up soft jazz on the sound system. At seven-o-five, my cell phone chirps. I buzz Jasmine into the lobby, prop the front door open with a brick, and make my way to the elevator to escort her up.

The ride up is a little awkward, like we haven't seen each other in quite some time, even though the opposite is true. As we move through the lobby and into the apartment, Jasmine stops, looks down, and says, "Nice doorstop."

"There's a story behind that brick."

"You'll have to tell me about it over drinks."

"Chilled vodka with fresh-squeezed lime juice okay with you?"

"Sounds great," replies Jasmine as I watch her take in the long, sparse, rectangular space. The soft light of late October—and corresponding shadows—falls across pillars and flooring.

"This place is amazing. I like that you didn't overdo it."

"You're kidding, right?" I say, as I fill two tumblers with vodka and juice before giving them a quick stir with a clean butter knife.

"No, I'm not joking. I like open space. Now, please tell me the story about the brick."

"It's really a story about my dad. He's dead, and I never really liked him much. But every once in a while he'd surprise me with drunken words of wisdom."

"I'm sorry to hear he passed."

"Don't be sorry. I didn't mean to start the night off on a depressing note, but he was not a good guy. The brick story was something he told me in a drunken rage. Yet it's one of those few life-advice nuggets that I got from him that actually made sense, at least to me. I still buy into the message today and try to practice it in my everyday life. I even shared it with Isabella."

"I really want to hear it now," replies Jasmine as she sips at her cocktail.

After taking a heavy pull on my drink, I say, "Okay, here goes. My dad would come home from work every night and proceed to get blasted. On his days off he'd do the same thing, starting at five in the evening. Never before five. He was adamant about that. I guess he figured if he started drinking at cocktail hour then he must not be an alcoholic. Anyway, one time when I was about seven or eight, he asked me a question after he's half in the bag and on his way to oblivion. He holds up a brick, not the one I have, but another brick that he got from who-knows-where. Like I said, he holds up this brick and shouts, 'Jack, what is this?' Again, I'm pretty young and totally caught off guard. I look up and I tell him it's a brick. My answer sends him into a head-shaking fury as he launches into this rant about how it's not just a brick. I only see it as a brick. He tells me he can name a bunch of things it could be other than a brick.

"I'm still staring at him and he says, 'I can name ten different things right now.' I'm speechless, scared, and he's looking at me like I just don't get it. Because I don't. Finally, in a stupor, he overdoes it with drunken theatrics by counting— out loud, as in shouting—while pulling down individual fingers. 'One: It could be a doorstop. Two: a hammer. Three: a weapon. Four: a steppingstone. Five: a dam in a small creek.' After rattling off the first five examples, he looks around the room as if he's lost, then puts the brick down on the coffee table so he can continue counting with his other hand. He's fading away and can't quite figure out how to simply pass the brick from one hand to the other or to just count to ten using the same five fingers.

"Then he starts up again, counting on the other hand, but in his condition it's becoming more and more difficult. 'Six: a paperweight. Seven: a shot put. Eight: a mini-shelf. And ten: a toy caboose.' When he's done counting, he looks at his fingers, confused, not sure if he's missed a number, looking around until he spots the brick on the coffee table. Finally, he focuses his attention back on me, screaming, 'Jack, use that fucking head of yours. Things aren't always what they appear to be. They can be other things, too. Think, son. For fuck's sake, think.'

"At that young age, and as scared as I was, I almost started laughing because I knew he'd fucked up on his numbers. It took everything in me to stand there with a straight face. But that was his brilliant lesson. Even while impaired, he made a good point. Don't just focus on the obvious. Sometimes the answers to your questions are right in front of you in the form of a brick. Sometimes objects, people even, are other than what they appear to be. I don't know why that stuck with me at such a young age, but it did. Anyway, that's what I took from his rant. I keep a brick as a reminder of the bizarre wisdom shared with me by my drunk and now dead father."

"That is a sad story, Jack. But a good story. Thanks for sharing it with me."

"No problem," I reply as I prepare another round of drinks.

Jasmine follows me out to the roof and watches as I flip and poke seasoned steaks. "Is medium-well okay?" I ask.

"Perfect," she replies.

The sexual tension is off the charts, at least on my end. I feel like a teenager on a first date, wanting to act cool but realizing I'm out of my league.

TWENTY-ONE

JACK

From grill to serving platter go the steaks as we walk back into the apartment, landing at the kitchen table.

"Steak and wine are all I've got. Do you want me to microwave a potato?" I ask.

"No, don't bother. Steak and wine will be fine."

"After dinner, my dessert will knock your socks off," I boast.

"What's for dessert?"

"A surprise."

We eat and drink and talk, asking pertinent questions, feeling each other out. After dinner, I remove the dinnerware from the kitchen table and stack it in the sink. I retrieve two coffee mugs from a cabinet and set them on the kitchen counter. Digging into a cold carton, I place two rounded scoops of vanilla bean Gelato inside the mugs—followed by two ounces of cold brew—before topping off the whole shebang with a heaping tablespoon of fresh whipped cream, grated dark chocolate, and a final splash of cold brew. "Let me know what you think," I say, handing over the dessert and eagerly watching as she readies herself for sweetness.

"What do you call this?" she asks, taking a spoonful of creamy dessert and slowly placing it in her mouth.

"It's called a Messy Machado. I stole the recipe from a friend of the Professors who lives down on the central coast in a town called Pismo Beach. The guy serves this same dessert at a coffeehouse called The Mad Azorean. The only difference, he uses espresso instead of cold brew."

"Oh my god, this is amazing," says Jasmine, as she proceeds to devour the dessert. Once she's eaten the whole thing, she pleads, "Please teach me how to make this."

"I will on our second date."

At the kitchen sink, I wash, she dries. The dishes are done and put away quickly.

Lounging in the front room, I pose the question, "Now what?"

"I don't want to sound out of line, or too forward, but I'd like to sleep with you, Jack. Not tonight, but eventually. I have some questions to ask first. One: Do you have any diseases I need to know about? Two: If you say you don't, are you willing to get tested to prove it? And three: Will sleeping with me be a problem for you at work? Because, you see, I don't want a boyfriend in the traditional sense, and it will most likely be a temporary situation."

I pause in thought, delighted she's gotten right to the point. In my mind, all relationships are negotiations, usually taking too much time, months, even years, to get things right. "I like people who just put it out there," I finally reply. "I don't have any diseases, and yes, I'll get tested to prove it. Also, I don't think having a monogamous relationship with you will be a problem for me at work because we'll only see each other on Sundays and we'll keep it professional. Business is business."

"The monogamous part will be your part. I also see someone else. A woman. I will only see you and her if you agree to the arrangement. And, if you're wondering about a threesome, the answer is no. I like both sexes, but I keep my relationships separate. Please give it some thought. If you agree, it'll stay between me and you. It will be absolutely nobody else's business: not friends, not family, not anybody's. If you can give me an answer in a few days, that would be great."

"I can give you an answer right now if that's okay with you."

"Let's hear it."

"Let's give it a try," I say.

"Great. Let me know when you get your test results back."

"I will do that," I reply, still a little perplexed that I've just entered into a relationship with a stunning woman whom I barely know and who happens to have a girlfriend on the side. I feel extremely excited about this new thing, this thing that reeks of lust and temporary commitment. I'm willing to try something different.

As Jasmine gets ready to leave, I ask if I can kiss her. She approaches and leans into me, her right hand barely touching my beltline. We share a long, sensuous kiss; and, when done, briefly look into each other's eyes. "I'll see you when I see you," I say, ending the silence.

"Yes, you will," purrs the pianist, walking away from the apartment, knowing full well I'm watching her slightly exaggerated hip movement as she sways into the waiting elevator. *Down she goes*, is my first thought. Followed by *Time for another shower.*

TWENTY-TWO

MONICA MARTINEZ

I sensed something was wrong. They were late. Way late, as I watched a police cruiser park outside our Brooklyn home.

I was barely a teenager, two weeks new to thirteen, when told my parents were dead. Killed in a car accident. Here, then gone. Simple as that.

My mother, Maria Martinez, had no surviving family members. Like me, she was an only child with dead parents. My father, Manuel Martinez, also with deceased parents, had one surviving sibling, a brother, my Uncle Pete—a Vietnam vet living the lonely life in a rented room over in Harlem.

Dead parents, left with one surviving relative, and lucky, I guess. Tell that to a teenager when you bring her the most devastating news of her life. Tell her she's lucky. Lucky. Whatever that's supposed to mean.

Social services, here I come. I sensed something else: I was not willing to readily embrace that future.

At first, I got moved around a lot. But at least I stayed in Brooklyn. I was also fortunate that none of my foster parents tried to fuck me, literally. That said, some of them were difficult as hell and had no business in that business because of an inability to care . . . their biggest sin. I also caught another break; meaning, I didn't get turned out or end up on dope. I'd heard the terrible stories. Seen some of it: drugs, prostitution, homelessness, and the crazy shit that comes with all three.

Those first four years after their deaths were a blur. Uncle Pete was my one constant, stopping by monthly like clockwork to hang out with me, right up until I turned seventeen. Uncle Pete was cool. He loved me, and felt guilty as hell that he couldn't be my legal guardian. But homeboy was dealing with mental issues and barely surviving as a swing-shift janitor at a high-rise in Manhattan. A union janitor, but still, like I said, barely surviving.

He would've kept visiting, but he died too. With no family except for me, no friends but me, he died alone. I wish I could have been there at the end to hold his hand, to tell him that I loved him. Another crushing death. I hope my parents and Uncle Pete are doing fine wherever they are. Not like some religious idea of the afterlife but rid of life's turmoil and given the chance to rest in peace.

I miss our monthly get-togethers. Uncle Pete coming over and taking me out to lunch, giving whatever foster parents I had at the time "the look." He was always mannered, but never overdid politeness. But like I said, he had this convincing look. Like maybe he'd seen or done some shit when he was in that war, and if anybody fucked with me, there was a high probability they were going to end up worse off for it.

Every time he left, he did so with tears in his eyes, apologizing for not having the skills or the wherewithal to raise me. I tried to reassure him, telling him it was going to be okay, that I'd get by. He'd look away, eventually looking back with sad eyes before hugging me and walking off—a straight-line to the subway station to catch a train home. He felt for me, as I did him, witnessing his hurt, his damaged being, his endless suffering.

Uncle Pete yearned to be left alone, wanting to exist unbothered. And when I say left alone, I mean left alone. That's exactly what I wanted. Too many people from social services couldn't comprehend that concept, acting as if they wanted to help. But it was just that—an act—as they smothered me with niceties lacking substance. But like Uncle Pete used to tell me, "Nice is just a tactic; a simple and often effective tactic." The other thing he used to say: "Get out of New York as soon as you can and head out to San Francisco." He always said I was going to make it wherever I went, so I might as well do it in better weather.

Uncle Pete left me his entire life savings. Some people would think it wasn't much. To me, it was a fortune, especially when combined with my parents' life insurance money. He also left a letter suggesting what to do with the money after leaving New York and venturing west. In that letter as well, solid life advice. Thank you, Uncle Pete.

I turned eighteen a month before graduating high school. I was a legal adult. No more social services. At exactly midnight, the second it was official, I packed all my shit into a large suitcase and left that foster-fucked house for the final time . . . never to step foot in a place like that again.

I couch-surfed with acquaintances for a few weeks; at last, graduating. In the end, I gathered my bags, hailed a cab, and left the Big Apple—choosing not to look back. Goodbye to no one in particular.

TWENTY-THREE

MONICA MARTINEZ

From JFK to Oakland on Jet Blue. I'm on a plane for the first time. After landing at the Oakland airport, I take a bus over to what they call BART, the West Coast version of a subway station. I pass under the bay in a tube—dark, eerie, noisy—just me and my stuff and a bunch of strangers. Same old, same old. From station, to stairs, to surfacing in San Francisco. Voilà: the bay, and a bridge named after that bay. My new home.

I check into a Holiday Inn Express, with prior reservations made with the thought of staying for a week, maybe two. I use my only credit card, the one Uncle Pete advised that I get: the one funded by my own money. I'll be paying in cash when I leave, having six grand stuffed down the front of my pants in a Ziploc bag. But for some things, you need a credit card. The way of the world, I guess. Uncle Pete used to say: "Use the card at least once a month for necessary purchases. But remember, pay it off each month in full so the banks don't tack on interest. Because that's what they want to do."

I head out of the hotel and wander into the first electronics store I see. I buy a laptop and a cell phone, getting a number with a San Francisco area code. Almost feeling like a California resident, I make my way over to a UPS store and rent a mailbox. For ID purposes, this will be my future address. On top of that, my mail will be safe and I'll have access to it most hours of the day. If I change residences—something my life has revolved around since I lost my parents—it will not matter because my mail drop and ID will stay the same.

That done, I hit up four established banks, opening accounts and depositing a hundred grand into each of the first three and fifty-seven thousand dollars and change into the fourth: all cashier's checks from my Brooklyn bank. My money will be protected and insured. All interest earned from the big three will be transferred into the smaller one once a year. Uncle Pete told me that banks insure your money up to a certain amount and not a penny more. Simple research proves him correct.

I'm not so concerned about making money with my money as much as I fret about losing it. I need to learn more about money. But at least it's mine. Like Uncle Pete said, "You'll be liquid, which means you can access your money whenever you want without asking for permission or paying unnecessary penalties."

On the way back to the hotel, I stop at an independent coffeehouse with a "Now Hiring" sign hanging in the front window. I fill out a job application and ask for the person in charge. Once he shows up, I hand over my application while making direct eye contact and offering a firm handshake. He responds in kind.

Back at the hotel, I go online and search for a place to live. Tomorrow I'll apply for a California ID and check out some studio apartments. Once again, thank you, Uncle Pete.

As the clock strikes nine, I'm standing in line at the California DMV. I complete the appropriate paperwork, have my picture taken, and get out of there after two hours of hurry up and wait—entangled in a bureaucratic trap that should've taken no more than twenty minutes. My new California ID will arrive in the mail soon enough. Officially a California resident, I grin ever so slightly before heading off to an appointment with one of several prospective landlords.

I'm dead tired when I trudge toward my final appointment of the day. I meet up with an older white dude—the property owner. The only way to describe the guy is that he's cool and calm and seems honest. We talk and walk as he shows me an old mechanic's garage converted into five studio apartments. He's asking five hundred dollars a month for the studio apartment—the smallest of the bunch, with first and last month's rent up front. If I agree and pay up, I can have the place in a few days after it's painted and new flooring is installed.

Stating that he rarely experiences turnover, he welcomes me to talk with the other tenants and adds that it's a first-come, first-serve deal. The place is barely three hundred square feet, and in its limited space are living quarters, a kitchen, a bathroom, a stackable washer/dryer and a closet. My take: efficient, clean, and enough room for me.

He's no sucker, though. Rent is due by the third of the month, and, if late, a ten-percent penalty is tacked on at straight up midnight. On top of that, if the rent isn't in his hands by the tenth of the month, paid in full plus penalties, he'll take your lack of action as a thirty-day notice and you're out of there at the end of the month.

Sold. I hand him a thousand dollars; intuition hinting that I'll be living here for a good chunk of time He gives me a receipt and a set of keys to both the building's entrance and my future unit, telling me it's mine and I can move in after repairs are completed in two or three days. Time to buy a bed and other essential crap.

TWENTY-FOUR

MONICA MARTINEZ

My cell phone chirps just as I reach the hotel. I look at the incoming number; it's coming from the coffeehouse where I filled out the job application. I answer the call. The person on the other end lets me know that if I want the job, I have an interview the following morning with the shop manager, a person he refers to as Big Sandy. I want the interview.

Once in my room, I break out the iron and put a detailed pressing on my only pant suit. It's basically my job interview, funeral, wedding, and important meeting wardrobe all rolled into one: black pants with matching coat, white blouse, black shoes, good manners. Here I come.

The following day, I meet with Big Sandy. I'm fifteen minutes early with a freshly printed résumé in hand, the contents of which are sparse. Big Sandy isn't as big as her nickname depicts, but she's not small either. The interview takes place right there in the main part of the coffeehouse, not in an office but at a table where customers sit. Maintaining eye contact, I respond to her questions with what I think are well thought-out answers. After forty-five minutes of talking and a tour of the place, she asks if I can commit to a thirty-two-hour work week starting the next day. I say I can. She tells me to meet her at the coffeehouse the following morning at four to learn opening procedures. I shake her hand and say, "I'll see you in the morning." She holds the handshake longer than usual to ask, "Is there any shift you can't work?"

"I'm open to any shift—any time, any day," is my speedy reply.

As she lets go of my hand, she says, "I'm gonna hold you to that, Monica."

Out the door I go, with more than a hint of confidence in my step, as if I've won the lottery. I've been in town three days, all the while following Uncle Pete's advice. Wise advice that proves to be solid. Of note, though, I have to keep my hustle on and work my butt off. No slacking off or letting my guard down. "Chill and come back down to earth," I say to myself.

The next morning, at ten minutes to four, I meet Big Sandy outside The Blue Bean coffeehouse. As I approach, she nods and opens with, "Good morning." I return her greeting. Big Sandy pulls out a set of keys and says, "I'm going to explain every little detail to you for at least a week. Don't think I'm insulting your intelligence because I'm not. Starting week two, you'll explain everything to me before you actually do it. Then you'll do it while I observe. I will be your teacher and your sounding board. If you don't remember something, or if you need clarification, just ask. This is the way I teach. My main objective is for you to learn correctly. Good habits, good performance."

I like Big Sandy's style. Here we go, coffeehouse one-oh-one.

The next two months fly by. I'm opening the shop, closing the shop, and doing everything asked of me. Being a top-notch barista and pouring a quality cappuccino is not an easy task. It takes practice, especially fine-tuning the correct texture, the right coloring, the overall aesthetic. And if you want to throw some art on top of that marbled milk canvas, well, you really have to know your shit. I'm not quite there yet. But like Big Sandy says as she asks me to go unclog a backed-up toilet, "If it was easy, they wouldn't call it work."

My hard work pays off. I'm working a consistent forty-hour work week at The Blue Bean, plus an additional six hours on Saturday mornings pedaling coffee with Big Sandy at the farmers' market. And just like Uncle Pete told me to do, I put ten percent of everything I earn into one of my savings accounts. The last time I met with Uncle Pete, about three weeks before he died, he rambled on about life and death and what I thought to be other unrelated nonsensical stuff. I wasn't quite sure what he was getting at. At times, I thought he was talking about my parents. But after his death, I thought maybe his ramblings were about himself, that he knew he was living on borrowed time. However, after a few months in San Francisco, I've changed my mind altogether. Because maybe, just maybe, he was actually talking about me. It was like he was challenging my intellect, my thinking, and telling me to be aware of not only my surroundings but also the ridiculousness of the world. A world that pecks away and hovers about patiently while wearing you down until you're at the point of giving up. His warning was, "Don't believe the lies, and don't live your life based on those lies—lies attached to mainstream everything."

One Saturday morning, while standing at the end of a vacant pier, I look out across the bay. There it is in all its glory:

The Golden Gate Bridge. I scan from left to right. No fog. No marine layer. Just a strong wind and clear blue skies for miles. Big Sandy asks if I've ever walked across it. I tell her I haven't. She says I should. I say I will, and never think too much about it until I do.

112

TWENTY-FIVE

JACK

My uncle is true to his word, ensuring that my immediate colleagues are free from unnecessary interference. However, those at *The City Wrap*—more to the point, the owner, and his star writer—are wide open to my uncle's full-time attention.

A second article in *The City Wrap* portrays the assistant chief as a tyrant focused on selfish wants, while at times ignoring the law. In addition, an internal affairs investigation is launched by the chief due to pressure from the mayor. The investigation of a high-ranking cop by fellow cops is more a covering of ass than anything else. Cops don't tend to investigate their brethren with full vigor and intensity, especially when the outcome of the investigation could spell disaster for the careers of those doing the investigating.

I'm sure my uncle is furious at himself for underestimating Rosenbaum and Smith. I'm guessing he'll be tiptoeing from the spotlight, allowing the heat to dissipate. Any thoughts of running for mayor are probably out of the question now. It appears as if he's peaked on the career ladder. A tough pill to swallow, I'm sure. Time for him to lie low. But forgive and forget? I don't see that happening, which is disturbing. I need to protect my loved ones, my friends, my mom—especially since I'm responsible for getting her involved in this whole mess.

Life returns to somewhat normal as the tension unleashed by my uncle subsides. There's a new tension lingering, though. A sexual tension. After getting a clean bill of health from my doctor, I share the results with Jasmine one afternoon prior to her second set in front of another packed house. "Next Sunday night is free for me as long as you can fit me into your busy schedule," she says. Without checking my calendar, I announce, "My schedule is wide open that night." A week to think about our next encounter is much too long.

I've had sporadic success with women. I tend to pick punishers and disciplinarians. The kind of women who, when things don't go their way and if I don't react properly in certain situations, believe I need to be taught a lesson. I've been sent home, denied sex, told to give serious thought about my untimely blunders and lack of caring, and to call back the following day to see if the relationship can be mended. I never call back. It's easier that way, not worth the effort to continue on. Fortunate or unfortunate, I've mastered the art of the walk-away-and-don't-look-back.

With one ex, she showed up at my place without warning weeks after our breakup, calling from the lobby of my building and saying that she needed to see me . . . that it was an urgent matter. I buzzed her up because I'm a sucker. As soon as she walked in, dropping her purse on the floor, she proclaimed, "I'm here to sleep with you for the final time. I want to give you a taste of what you'll be missing going forward." It turns out she was partially right. It was great sex, sex to be missed.

The kicker is, I don't miss her. Big ocean, plenty of fish.

I don't think I'm the long-term relationship type. Is that a bad thing? I honestly don't know. Jasmine appears to be different in a good way. All she really wants is a part-time relationship with limited strings attached. That's what I've always thought I wanted. Now I have it, and it scares the shit out of me even though it's barely begun. Life is a caustic bitch sometimes.

However, thoughts of Jasmine put crazy fears on hold. To me, it feels like the first time I bungee jumped off a bridge. As I stood alone, hovering at the edge, one-hundred-eighty-seven feet above a rushing river in the Northern California foothills, I thought to myself, *What the fuck?*, and jumped. With Jasmine, I'm teetering again.

TWENTY-SIX

ALLEN SMITH

I stop at my usual early morning hang, a Chinese restaurant/donut shop four blocks from work. Breakfast: a large black coffee and two jelly-filled donuts. I'm not paying much attention when I leave the sugar shop. No reason to. If I'd been aware, I would have noticed before now that I'm being followed. The man tailing me finally nerves up to make the approach. I catch motion out of the corner of my eye as I veer onto a street not far from work. My pursuer gets closer.

Not fucking around, I stop and turn toward him— aggressively quickening my pace. If I'm about to die, I'm gonna go down fighting. Ten feet out, ready to throw hot coffee and a barrage of punches, recognition sinks in. I haven't seen James in quite some time. Didn't know he was still alive. We stop within inches of each other.

Surrendering by putting his hands in the air, James says, "I'm sorry if I spooked you, but I need your help." Caught in close range of the addict's stench, I take a step back, knowing all too well that my little brother has asked for help hundreds of times before; not from me, but from our parents. I also know that James, a sibling I've spent little time with because of a sizable age gap, was spoiled rotten and given everything by our parents. In return, he gave them a huge dose of grief and disappointment right up to their dying days, three weeks apart from one another. James stole from, lied to, and verbally abused our mom and dad most of his life. For some reason, they always forgave him, always offering hope for their unplanned baby boy.

I see something different in his eyes, like he thinks he has a shot at change. But my longtime beat-writer's sense reminds me I'm dealing with an addict, a thief, a liar, a con.

"What kind of help, James?"

"Rehab help. I gotta quit or I'm gonna die."

"Everybody dies. That's guaranteed. How many rehabs have you been to in the last fifteen years?"

"Seven or eight."

"What's the longest amount of time you've stayed sober?"

"A couple of months," replies James.

I give him a look of disappointment, shaking my head from side to side, before saying, "I'll see what I can do. But if I help you, it'll be a one-time thing. If you fail again, I'll walk away and ignore the rearview mirror. I'm not Mom and Dad. They were decent folks, and you fucked them over."

He fidgets, rubbing his hands together as if he's cold, but maintains eye contact. I don't remember James being that guy. He's always been a lie-and-look-away sort of dude. "If I help you, *IF*, you're gonna have to leave the city. So, basically, it'll be up to you and whatever it is that gets people like you sober. Meet me at the donut shop tomorrow morning at eight and be prepared to leave the city. If you don't show up, it'll be no skin off my ass, bro."

"I'll be there."

I watch my little brother, a brother I barely know, turn and walk away.

It breaks my heart.

120

TWENTY-SEVEN

JASMINE

Walking through Potrero Hill, I cruise up a steep incline at a decent pace on a street named after a ship named after the smallest state in the country. I approach his house, skip the knocking part, open the front door, and step inside. I call out his name as I close the door. Ricky Ruth leans out from the kitchen and says, "You are one on-time woman."

The top floor of the tri-level is a private living quarters with a dominant staircase leading upward—stained oak and black steel. The street level apartment is Ricky Ruth's, which includes a narrow, carpeted stairway leading down to a basement flat housing a state-of-the-art recording studio with just enough room for a four-piece band to squeeze into. The best part of the basement is concealed at the bottom of a wooden trunk: high-grade magic mushrooms grown in and harvested from sterile jars.

Ricky Ruth hands me a vacuumed-sealed plastic bag and says, "Two medium doses of the best Ecuadorian caps and stems for the little lady," as if a conversation between shop owner and customer has just taken place.

"Thanks, Ricky Ruth. I really appreciate it," I say, handing over the agreed-upon amount.

"No worries, Jazzy Jaz. Would you like a cup of tea?"

"Sure."

We head into the kitchen and sit at a bright yellow 1950s-style table situated within an alcove. I look out a window that reveals a city backyard no bigger than the table, where potted plants rest on mossy brick. "Who are the zoomers for?" asks Ricky Ruth.

"Me and a friend. At least I think so. I really don't know if he'll partake."

"I'm sure if you ask nicely and throw in a 'pretty please', he'll play along, little lady."

"You may be right about that, Ricky Ruth."

We both have busy schedules, so, after tea, we wrap matters up with hugs and air-kisses, saying our goodbyes. Ricky Ruth goes down to the basement and the confines of the recording studio while I step out the front door.

TWENTY-EIGHT

ALLEN SMITH

I arrive at the donut shop two hours early and order my usual combination of fat, sugar, and caffeine. I select a booth facing the shop's front window; a bench, really, covered in faded orange vinyl, with direct views of the comings and goings. Once situated, I peruse several out-of-state newspapers—a morning ritual. Ten minutes before the agreed meet time, I spot my sibling approaching from across a busy street. I fumble with my cell phone before finally sending a two-word text.

Shortly thereafter, James enters the donut shop, spots me straight away, and walks over to the booth. I look up at him and then down at the empty seat directly across from me. Slowly registering the nonverbal communication, James places his underweight body on the plastic seat and slides over. Just as he settles in, a car pulls up to the curb and out steps a large, menacing figure with ex-biker mannerisms and leatherwear tightly fitted over a muscled frame. The car pulls away as the biker dude enters the shop and walks up to our table.

The large man looks down at James and asks, "Mind if I take a seat?"

Confused, James looks at me.

"Move over. He's here to meet you and vice versa." As the big fella wedges into the booth, I make the introductions. "James, Monty. Monty, James."

Monty sticks out a large paw and James shakes his hand with a limp hand.

Monty says, "Pleased to meet you. Now let's get down to business. I understand that you want to quit the old life and get clean and sober, as we say."

James manages a low volume, "Yeah, that's right."

"Perfect. Well, this all begins with honesty. I say that because I have a few questions for you. So, your undivided attention and the truth will help move things along. Now if you choose to lie to me, and most addicts do, then you aren't coming with me and your brother here won't be out a bunch of hard-earned cash that he seems willing to part with on your behalf. Do you understand what I'm saying?"

"Yeah."

"Great. When was the last time you got high?

I interrupt. "Dude, I don't care if you're high right now. Just answer honestly so we can get you where you need to be."

James gives me a slight nod, turns toward Monty, and says, "I got high about a half hour ago."

"Cool. What are you currently on?"

"A little black-tar and some vodka."

"Got it," replies Monty. "Now, here's the bigger ask. I need everything you have on your person." Monty pulls out a sealable plastic bag from inside his leather coat. "Hear me out on this. I don't care if you've got dope, booze, weapons, or whatever hidden on your body. But I'm gonna need all of it before I take you to a decent place to catch a shower and get some clean clothes. I know you need to detox for a week or so, and my partner, who happens to be a nurse, is going to give you a little something-something for the trip we're about to take if you decide to do the right thing." Monty stops talking and looks around the donut shop. He starts up again, this time whispering, "If, for whatever reason, you have something hidden up your ass, please do not take that out here. I can't emphasize that point enough. Just tell me what it is and we, I mean you, can do the ass retrieval thing when you're in the shower. So, give me what you've got. But tell me what it is first before you start pulling shit out."

James says, "First of all, I don't hide stuff up my butt. Never have. That said, here goes. I have an empty syringe in my pocket." He does a personal pat-down on his right front pants pocket. "I have a half-pint of vodka in my right sock. A knife and my ID are in my back pockets. That's it. That's all I've got. Oh, and a pack of cigarettes and a joint in my left sock."

Monty opens the plastic bag and says, "Place the needle and the knife and the smokes and your ID in the bag. Be careful with the needle." After James does as he's told, Monty continues, "Now, pull the vodka out." James retrieves the half pint of vodka and sets it on the table. There's an inch of clear liquid inside. Monty says, "Go ahead and drink that." James looks at Monty as if he's about to be tricked. Monty adds, "Hopefully, that's your last drink. So, either drink up or give it to me. It's not going to change your sobriety date one way or the other." James quickly twists the cap off the bottle and downs the cheap booze in a hurried gulp. Monty reaches out with the plastic bag and James drops the empty bottle inside.

"Are you holding anything else? Anything at all, because

this is your last chance."

"Nothing. I gave you everything. I'm ready to go. Let's do this."

"Cool. Now say goodbye to your brother," replies Monty while sending a text.

James looks at me and says, "Thanks for the help. I won't let you down, bro."

I wonder how many times James said those exact words to our parents. The same tired lines. The same lies. The same old shit. My response to my brother is like that of a Vegas card dealer: "Good luck."

The same car from earlier pulls up to the curb. Monty squeezes out of the booth and motions for James to go ahead of him. From booth to worn linoleum to out the front door and into a foreign car goes James, with the burly recovering addict right behind him. As the car drives off, I take a sip of coffee before looking down at a stack of newspapers, all the while holding back decades of emotions.

TWENTY-NINE

ASSASSIN

The fourth package arrives three days after the third package. I received the first and second packages a week ago; two days apart from one another. In total, the packages were sent to four different addresses. Each package contains one piece of the puzzle, except for the final package, which contains two. Combine all five pieces and you have a killing device that fits inside the average adult male's hand: frame, slide, spring, grips, clip. The weapon, a .22 caliber semi-automatic pistol, is a finely crafted, German-machined beauty. My weapon of choice. A small caliber gun means not a lot of noise, and if everything goes as planned, the bullet hits the desired target without exiting. Instead, the cartridge, or cartridges, play the ricochet game while causing severe internal damage and, ultimately, death . . . the task at hand.

Patience is my strength—that and getting established and in place to close the deal. I clean the gun and assemble it to perfection. The bullets were purchased at a sporting goods store in Reno and paid for in cash. Paranoid? No. A skilled killing professional? Yes. The life-ending device, polished like a fine piece of silverware, is delicately set into a padded box. Through careful and disciplined preparation, the gun and bullets are free of fingerprints, of DNA. Now it's about waiting for the right opportunity. The right opportunity simplifies things; meaning being up close and trusted.

After recounting the agreed upon fee, I sink into a Saarinen Womb Chair and remove a Nat Sherman cigarette from the stylish confines of a designer case. I place the gold-filtered cigarette between ready lips and torch the black paper with a monogrammed lighter. I draw the first hit of high-end smoke into my lungs and hold it there. After three or four heartbeats, I exhale, followed by relaxed relief—putting my pace of mind into a lower gear. But not for long, because from this moment forward, it will be pure calculation and intensity up to the point of pulling the trigger. After that, a little time off before the next one.

THIRTY

JASMINE

Entering the refurbished storage space is like walking into an old church from years gone by; multiple candles alight and the smell of incense burning. I call out to an empty apartment. Within seconds, I hear a door shut out in the lobby, followed by Jack hustling through the front door. "There she is," he says, walking over, holding a corkscrew. He gives me a quick peck on the lips before adding, "I had to borrow this from the Professor. I have no clue where I stashed mine. By the way, you look beautiful."

I feel myself blush as I say, "Thank you." Still a little embarrassed, I turn and gaze toward the back of the apartment before asking, "Do you mind if I take a quick shower?"

Looking down at my travel bag, Jack answers, "Go ahead. Whatever you need."

"I'll do that," I reply, as I head for the shower situated behind a freestanding partition of see-through glass blocks.

The sound of water striking tile has to get his attention. My silhouette can be seen through steam and candlelight and shadows; the shower's spray, the water gliding down my body. He tells me later I was spot on, that he made a cocktail and parked himself in a chair, keenly observing the goings on at the far end of the apartment. Aroused and sitting in wait, he played the role of voyeur. I knew he was watching. I wanted him to.

I turn the water off and grab a towel hanging nearby. Still naked, I walk around the partition, make eye contact, and say, "Let's go to bed." Jack does as told, awkwardly fumbling out of his clothes.

Once on the bed, we explore. I whisper directions in his ear—how I like this, how I like that, sexual communication with a thoughtful assist. Silent, Jack follows along. The only sounds in the apartment are ours. Gentle, direct, and with a goal in mind, I take Jack through a tour of my body. In a sense, this is what works for me. Jack comes through and is rewarded with the sound of my release.

Relaxed and ready to reciprocate, I focus solely on Jack, asking relevant questions. Do you like this? You do. More? Sure. You're close. Come on, baby.

In the shower, we wash each other. Finished, we dry off. In robes and sipping cocktails, I ask, "Do you want to try some mushrooms?"

"Are you talking about the party kind of mushrooms?"

"I am."

"You have some?"

"I do."

"Are they any good?"

"The best, and they're extremely fresh."

"Sure, let's do it," says Jack.

From vacuum-packed plastic to hesitant mouths, we chew, chew, chew the earthy fungus before washing it down with fresh cocktails.

"How long does it take for these to kick in?" asks Jack.

"Less than thirty minutes," I reply, now an expert regarding Rickey Ruth's fun fungus.

We wait. We wait some more. Twenty minutes in, the subtleness of our upcoming journey begins. Off we go. A different feeling in the stomach, a slight tingle, followed by a heightened sensory sensation, followed by a deeper, extreme sensation of everything.

Pink Floyd is pulled up on the sound system, every candle blown out but one. The light from a single candle is more than ample as our pupils fully dilate.

We go our separate ways, each experiencing our own personal journey. Occasionally we meet up by a bookshelf, outside on the roof, lying on our backs in the lobby. We look at each other and bust out laughing, laughing so hard our stomach muscles ache. We stop laughing, catch a breath, then start laughing again, causing each other to go our separate ways yet again. This goes on for three hours before we start to come down from the mushroom high. After four hours, we're almost back to normal, still a little tipsy and full-on naked. Back to bed we go.

I wake up in the morning with a wine glass in my hand, causing me to think about a Peter Frampton song. I start to laugh but quickly suppress it due to excruciating pain, as if I'd done sit-ups all night. I look around the bed, then the apartment, but he's nowhere to be found. I look at the front door and notice it's propped open. I hope he's out getting coffee and bagels.

Shortly thereafter, in walks Jack with a couple of coffees and a bag of food that smells wonderful. Famished, we dive into breakfast burritos. As we sit back and sip coffee, I ask,

"Did you have a good time last night?"

"No. I had a great time, even if I feel like I did a thousand crunches."

We both want to laugh, but the thought of more pain stifles that. "I had a great time, too. But, unfortunately, I have to get going."

"Use me and run. Is that how it's going to be?"

"This time it is," I reply, adding, "We'll have to do this again sometime." I grab my travel bag and make my way out the front door. Jack follows through the lobby, giving me a kiss on the lips before I leave. "See you around sometime, pretty lady."

I spank his ass and say, "You just might, sailor," as I step into the waiting elevator.

THIRTY-ONE

ALLEN SMITH

I peer through the peephole but don't recognize her. They change it up now and then and apparently this is one of those times. I open the door and invite her in. Like the others, she brings her own equipment. The portable massage tables are lightweight but strong framed, strong enough to support my bulk.

I'm a once-a-month customer, with everything arranged online. I guess that makes me a regular. She's attractive, slender, athletic in a middle-distance-runner kind of way. We exchange pleasantries then get down to business, as in four-hundred dollars, which will include a full body massage and a happy ending. While she speaks, I detect a slight accent but can't quite place it. Upper Midwest? Maybe.

Once the table is set up, I climb aboard—lying face down, wearing only a robe. The masseuse, after shedding her clothes, positions my arms and then pulls the top section of my robe down about halfway and begins the massage; a pair of highly skilled hands going to work on my upper body. She's strong, stronger than the others. Eventually, my robe is completely removed as she massages my entire backside. As instructed, I roll onto my back, immediately becoming aroused once I view her nakedness. She continues with the front-side portion of the massage, working all points of interest until I'm ready for completion. Like a master, she brings me to a satisfied conclusion, followed by a thorough clean-up with a soothing, warm washcloth.

When done, she asks if she can grab a smoke on the balcony.

"Sure, as long as I can bum a cig."

She hands me a cigarette, a brand I've never seen before. We make our way out to the balcony, smoking in total silence.

After extinguishing my smoke on the railing, I drop it on the deck and go inside to use the bathroom. While peeing, I feel completely relaxed, totally emptying my bladder without effort. With that out of the way, I go to say goodbye, but she's nowhere to be found. Must've been in a hurry.

Finding her sudden departure odd, I walk the entire apartment, looking in every room before finally making my way back to the balcony. Beautiful and gone, but for two cigarette butts. Like she was never here.

Tired, I secure the house, shutting and locking both the balcony slider and the front door. With heavy eyes, I go to bed, falling into a deep sleep not long after my head hits the pillow.

I suddenly wake and look at the glowing alarm clock. It's a little after three in the morning. Did I hear something, or dream I did? I still myself and listen. Something seems off.

I ease out of bed, kneeling on the carpeted floor. Quietly opening a nightstand drawer, I remove a powerful handgun, a revolver. With the gun at my side, I stand up and quietly walk to the bedroom door. A quick peek into the hallway reveals nothing. I walk that way until facing the bathroom head-on, less than fifteen feet away. To my right is the opening leading into the front room. At the brink of vacant space, I stop and take an angled look into the room, viewing roughly half of it. I don't see anything out of the ordinary. Summoning courage, I quickly walk the entire exposed span until reaching the other side. I immediately turn back around and shoot an angled glance into the portion of room I missed on the first go-around. Still nothing of concern. Pivoting one-hundred-and-eighty degrees, I focus my attention on the bathroom. As I stand there staring and listening, what I hear doesn't seem right. It's more pronounced, like wind pushing through a thicket.

Walking into the bathroom, I focus on the shower enclosure. I observe nothing unusual as I peer at the milky plastic door . . . no shadows, no human form, no movement whatsoever. I slide it open anyway, revealing an empty tub and an open window, a window that's remained open for years. Suddenly, the hair on the back of my neck stands on end. I slowly turn around, raising the gun. Again, nothing. However, it's now quite obvious to me the normal audio levels in the flat have been altered—a different kind of white noise. I take a deep breath before continuing.

Leaving the bathroom, I walk through the hallway and into the front room, quickly giving it the once-over. Within seconds, I recognize the anomaly. The sliding glass door leading out to the balcony is wide open, causing a cross draft. I don't remember it being open when I glanced at it two minutes earlier. I also know for a fact that I shut and locked it before I went to bed. Gun at the ready and my head swiveling, I walk out onto the balcony, knowing full well whoever was there will be gone. Searching every inch of the deck proves my intuition correct. The two cigarette butts from the previous night are nowhere to be found. Not a fleck of tobacco, as if the deck has been swept clean. Those unique gold filters have disappeared. She didn't want to leave anything behind.

Walking to the front door, I check the deadbolt. Unlocked. I take a few steps to the kitchen to check the nearest drawer. The key is gone. Shaking my head in disbelief, I realize how stupid I am for storing my only spare key in a drawer no more than ten feet from the front door.

I lock the door, power up my cell phone, and do a search for an all-night locksmith. *Could've been worse* is my first thought. Fresh coffee and new locks are my second and third thoughts as I make my way back to the kitchen and over to the coffeemaker.

THIRTY-TWO

JASMINE

I awake to a soft touch, rolling over and facing my lover. After embracing, we kiss. Done with the first kiss, I ask, "Where've you been?"

"Just out and about."

We quit talking, falling into a rhythm; a rhythm I've never experienced with any other lover. Our physical forms come together just right, move just right, touch just right. Pure knowing, efficient motion.

Still, I know little about this other woman. Sure, I've had a key to her place for some time, but her place reveals nothing. It's basically sterile. Not quite. But close. Nice, simple things. Better than nice, actually; all high-end and modern. However, the telling of anything substantial is nonexistent, with never a mention of the city or town she's from—or family, or career. Mysterious.

I never think to pry. Not knowing is the main reason the relationship works. That was the initial hook. There's an excitement to it. A comfortable unknown. It's a huge turn-on for me. I assume it's the same way for her.

So, I play along. Oh, and those strong yet gentle hands.

THIRTY-THREE

ISABELLA

My mom and I wade through the crowd at the busy Saturday morning farmers' market. A variety of sellers in mismatched booths spill across unmarked boundaries, their goods on display. From pour-over coffee to exotic jewelry and fresh organic vegetables, assorted merchandise and payment methods exchange multi-shaded hands. With the bay's shimmering water as a backdrop, there's a high energy, a good community feel to the bazaar-type atmosphere. It's always fun to hang out here.

Just as I take a sip of hot chocolate, I spot a familiar outline. Lowering my steamy drink, I slowly turn around, my back now facing him so he can't recognize me. It's definitely him—the man from school. But he isn't wearing a hat or sunglasses as he stands next to a police cruiser, chatting up a female cop in uniform.

Signaling to my mom that I'm on the move, I find a better place to spy, one where he can't get an unobstructed view of me. With my phone, I time it just right and snap off a series of pics. Satisfied that I still can't be seen, I make my way back to my mother and give her the look—the adolescent portrait of *I'm so, so bored that it's about to lower my life expectancy.*

She rolls her eyes, but quickly gives in. "Let's go grab lunch at The Hall." As we walk down Market Street, I send six pics to Matty Marshall, along with a message saying I'm safe, that I'm with my mom and we're on our way to The Hall to get our grub on. Matty responds right away, texting that he'll see me at The Hall after swinging by the Ferry Building to get a positive ID on someone he says he believes he already knows.

Sitting alone and waiting for lunch, my focus is on the front door when Matty strolls in. He spots me and comes over to the table, easing into a chair directly across from me. Holding up his cell phone, he slowly mouths, "Are you one-hundred percent positive this is the guy from your school?" I nod. Matty says, "This stays between me and you, nobody else. We never had this conversation and don't mention it in any future text messages."

I mouth, "Okay," then ask, "Are you going to take care of it?"

"As a matter of fact, I am. But it stays on the down-low from here on out. And I mean way down and way low."

I nod in agreement while extending a clenched hand. We bump fists, never to discuss it again.

As my mom brings food and drinks to the table, she sees Matty and asks, "Will you join us for lunch? It's on me."

Matty says, "No way I turn down lunch with two beautiful young ladies," as he winks the slyest of winks at me.

THIRTY-FOUR

ALLEN SMITH

Rosy had asked me to develop a feature story on Jasmine, her musical prowess, a mini-bio of sorts. Basically, a return favor to Jack for continuing to take out full-page ads in *The City Wrap*. Also, the young singer/pianist is forcing quite a few people to sit up and take notice. Word is getting out about her talent and looks, and readers are always hungry for what's new.

We agree to meet at The Hall after one of her performances. At the last minute, she lets me know via text that Mike Gates has agreed to whip up an early dinner for two. A table will be set up in the backroom just outside the kitchen door. We will dine in private without distraction and I can ask the needed questions to complete the article.

I show up early to catch her final set. After her performance, Jasmine walks into an unplanned meet-and-greet. Twenty minutes later, she moseys over, apologizing for the delay and telling me she'll meet me in back in five minutes. With that, she disappears.

I down another shot of tequila before making my way into

the backroom to find a long table covered in a brilliant white tablecloth, chairs positioned at opposite ends. Also on the table are sets of fancy silverware, matching cloth napkins, and white candles stationed in crystal candleholders. As soon as I take a seat, Jasmine comes through an exterior door with a bottle of wine in tow, saying, "I thought we'd drink something special with dinner tonight." Approaching the table, she hands me a bottle from a well-known Napa Valley winemaker. Repositioning her chair closer to me, she says, "I hope you like it."

After browsing the vintage year on the label, I say, "This is for us?"

"It most certainly is. If it wasn't for Jack and Ana and your paper, it would've taken who knows how long, if ever, for people to find out about me. And now you're giving me more free publicity."

Placing the bottle on the table, I say, "Since we're drinking this with dinner, I wouldn't exactly call my feature piece free. But heck, I'm all in. Have a seat and let's uncork this sucker."

In a flash, Mike Gates comes bustling through the swinging doors, flailing a corkscrew like a madman wielding a knife. Following in his wake are a mixture of delightful aromas that beg the question, "What's for dinner?"

With the wine uncorked, sampled, and poured, we clink glasses as I say, "L'chaim!" We sip and savor the aged red wine. The Lithuanian chef returns to the kitchen without uttering a word.

With the bottle half gone, Mike Gates reappears carrying salad plates and a loaf of warm sourdough bread, fresh from the oven. As he peppers the medley of greens, he finally speaks. "Take time. More courses come." Back to the kitchen goes the proud, focused chef.

The salads are followed by pumpkin soup. The soup gives way to the main course: a filet mignon roast served medium rare with steamed asparagus lightly brushed in an olive oil and lemon juice concoction. For dessert, we're treated to a freshly prepared chocolate soufflé drizzled with a tart raspberry sauce, with a sprinkling of powdered sugar on top. Accompanying the sugar extravaganza is a twenty-five-year-old tawny port. At last, fresh espresso arrives so we can have an in-depth conversation so I can complete the article.

"Why'd you move out to San Francisco?"

"To play music in the town where my father made his mark. To live where he settled. To get to know his side of my family."

Feeling an investigative twinge, I say, "I doubt that's the only reason you came out here."

"There is another reason. And it happens to be personal, something I don't want to talk about, something I wouldn't want made public. I don't know why I just shared that with you, but I trust that my explanation will stay between us. You appear to be an observant man when it comes to people and situations."

"Enough said. Forget about it. It was simply something I sensed. Sometimes shitty things happen to good people. It'll never be mentioned, written about, or brought up again." We talk at length about her musical training and she offers up a tidbit or two for inclusion in the article. My final question: "What direction do you want your career to go in?"

"I want to travel the world and support myself by playing music. Just like my father did. That would be my dream come true."

"That will happen for you. I'm not just saying that, either. You have what it takes and you have a certain style, a certain something that's quite attractive. And I'm not just talking about your looks. If there's anything I can do for you, ever, just let me know."

"That's really nice of you. Thank you. I feel lucky that you're the one writing this piece. It means a lot to me. When will it be in print?"

"I'll wrap it up tonight and send it over for editing. I've been working on it pretty steadily. I just needed some final thoughts from you, and now I have them. It'll be next week's feature story. You're not supposed to know about that, so keep it to yourself."

"Wow. That's really nice. Thanks, and my lips are sealed."

"Thank you for a lovely dinner. It was magnificent. Your presence made it wonderful."

"I owe you the thanks. So, let's leave it at that: a wonderful dinner, prepared by a wonderful chef, for two wonderful guests."

THIRTY-FIVE

ALLEN SMITH

I leave first, walking home along familiar streets. I can't remember the last time I felt this good. Once home, I take a quick shower, followed by a long, hard look in the mirror. I don't like what I see. I haven't shaved in three days and I'm in desperate need of a haircut. I'll take care of that in the morning. Sitting down at my desk, laptop ready, I rework the article for the umpteenth time, making last-minute changes—additions, deletions—before sending it off for editing. Tired, I call it a night and go to bed.

Sleeping soundly, I dream a dream that stays with me the next day. The details are sketchy, but the theme is ever-present in my memory: joy, deep love for family and friends.

The next morning as I sift through a stack of mail over a cup of coffee, I notice a postcard ad for fifty-percent off at an upscale barbershop, something I've received in the mail before. They're offering a deal on a shave and a haircut for twenty-five dollars; not "two bits" like the old ditty, but a haircut and straightedge razor shave, no less. Heck, and at a decent price.

In the shower. Out of the shower. I get dressed and head out the front door with the mailer in hand.

Upon arriving at a warehouse in the throes of renovation, I peek at the postcard, checking to see if I got the address right. I did. Entering the large structure, I pause to check things out. What lies before me are a multitude of construction projects in different stages of progress. A bevy of retail businesses are scattered about, with some completed and in full swing, while others are in disarray.

Coming around a bend, I find what looks to be an old-fashioned barbershop. It is an aesthetic wonderment, an eye-catching architectural cube no bigger than twenty-by-twenty feet. It's constructed out of dark, reddish-brown wood and paned glass. Its interior focal point is a 1930s-style barber chair positioned smack dab in the middle of the spotless shop. The place reminds me of a well-crafted fish tank with a human twist, giving those who walk by a three-sided view to peer inside, to be the voyeur as the barber trims away. An older Asian man, looking dapper in pressed slacks and a dress shirt, is seated in the burgundy-leather chair, an unlit cigarette dangling from his lower lip as he peruses the *Sporting Green*.

I open the door and walk inside. The old man looks my way, sizing me up before announcing, "You get shave and haircut."

I reply as if asked a question, saying, "Yes, shave and haircut," as I hand him the postcard.

All but ignoring the mailer, the old man hoists himself out of the custom chair, tosses the card on the nearest countertop, and offers up the chair with a single-handed gesture. I take a seat, inhaling the old-timey scent, admiring the shop's detailed craftsmanship. The old man reclines the barber chair, causing me to exhale and release the tension associated with letting a stranger cut your hair for the first time, quickly pushing back scary thoughts of a nicked face and a bowl cut. Within minutes, my face is wrapped in a steaming hot towel, and I begin to relax while thinking about the previous night's dream. As I continue to decompress, I suddenly doze off in the confines of leather and warmth and trusted aromas, as if safely secured in a silky cocoon.

Not knowing how long I've slept, I slowly wake to a familiar smell and the clicking of high heels on a solid floor. The smell: a distinct tobacco from an expensive cigarette. A brand inhaled not long ago.

In a fraction of a second, I think about how lucky I've been—able to do what I've always wanted to do, which is write and point out life's wrongs and rights and truths while making a decent living doing so. Then I think about how I've loved and been loved. That's enough, I think. My final thought.

It takes several minutes and several passersby before someone concludes that a lone man reclined in a barber chair with internal fluids leaking from his head is an oddity. Police are summoned. Once Smith is identified, a call to Rosenbaum is made. That prompts an all-out stampede of more cops, a shitload of reporters, and a sprinkling of rubberneckers wanting to witness the gore. By then, the assassin is long gone.

Once the body is covered and the crime scene secured, the lead detective calls the owner of the barbershop, dialing the number listed on a stray postcard. The owner seems confused because his shop isn't open for business on Mondays. Also, no one else is employed at the shop because it is a one-man operation. Aside from his wife, the shop owner is the only other person with a key. The detective doesn't give a shit about the owner's explanation and tells him to get his ass down to the shop or he'll personally come get him. The owner says he'll be there in a jiffy. *What the fuck is a jiffy?* thinks the detective as he abruptly hangs up.

Nobody really witnessed anything. Someone thought they saw an Asian or Hispanic guy wandering around. Age? *Not sure.* Height? *I don't remember.* Any specific physical characteristics? *Like what?* Tattoos or birthmarks or a 1970s porn mustache? *Are you serious?* Yeah, I'm serious. *I don't recall anything like that.* The detective thinks, *I'm not surprised.*

A young guy said he saw a really hot babe. What'd she look like? *You know, like hot, way hot.* How tall? *I think she was wearing heels.* So how tall? *I don't remember, but she was hot.* What else was she wearing? *Don't remember, but oh man, was she super-hot.* Nationality? *Could've been a lot of things. You know, maybe she was a mix.* What kind of mix? *A mix that made her hot.* Thanks for nothing.

The detective has serious thoughts about telling the young man to never have children until he improves his verbal skills, maybe adding a couple of two-syllable words to his vocabulary that have nothing to do with the word *hot*. Instead, he thinks, *fuck it*, and keeps his worldly observations to himself, just like his wife has been telling him to do for the past twenty-two years.

THIRTY-SIX

ROSENBAUM

The following day, I make the four-hour journey north to inform the next of kin—Smith's brother. With a rehab counselor present, I break the news to the younger Smith. As warned, James doesn't handle it well, probably feeling emotions he hasn't felt in years due to now being untainted by chemical numbing agents. I tell the living Smith that all costs are covered for however long he needs treatment. Also, if he ever returns to San Francisco and needs anything, like a job or a meal or a place to sleep, simply look me up and I'll help him out.

Once I leave, as I drive back to San Francisco, I finally weep, weeping for lost life, lost friendship, and the squandering of it all. With that out of the way, I get pissed off.

There's no funeral. Smith made sure of that with a rock-solid trust. Cremation followed by ashes spread in the bay beneath the famous bridge—illegal as hell—are in order with Smith's last wishes. Simple and to the point.

I organize an event for Smith at The Hall. Reporters, friends, some politicians, and acquaintances are invited.

Absolutely no cops will attend, with only a few asking. Matty was one of them, but he stayed away at my request.

With Smith's ashes in an urn stationed at center stage, his old friend, frontman and musician Barney Kellogg of the band Spangled Hash, plays an intense and somewhat comical version of a Frank Turner song, *The Ballad of Me and My Friends*. Later, Jasmine, with cello accompaniment from Kellogg, performs a Lindi Ortega tune, *So Sad*, leaving not a dry eye in the house. The alcohol flows.

The City Wrap puts out a special edition that week; a recent photo of Smith captured on the cover, his writing accomplishments listed next to a tight obit. The following week, Smith's final feature article is front page news. A black-and-white photo of Jasmine sitting at a piano takes up the entire front page.

In the end, life resumes . . . like it always does.

THIRTY-SEVEN

MATTY

I watch as the assassin returns to home base, probably needing to wrap up unfinished business. Upon opening, then closing the front door, she may have sensed my presence. Whether she did or she didn't, it doesn't change the outcome. The lightning-quick punch knocks her out cold. Then I give her a prick to the neck with a powerful sedative.

Hours later, the assassin slowly awakens, duct-taped to a steel chair bolted atop a concrete slab in a tiny room far away from where she lost consciousness.

Standing in front of her, I say, "Good evening."

The assassin does not respond, instead eyeing the dank surroundings. She has to be aware of the controlled breathing coming from a third person right behind her.

I wait, allowing her time to gather her bearings. "I'd introduce myself, but you and I both know that'd be a waste of time. You're probably wondering how I figured it out, how I know what you do for a living. You are a killer, just like me and the gentlemen sitting behind you."

I let my opening statement sink in before continuing. "We happen to be three different types of killers. Even so, killers through and through. The difference between you and me and my associate is that you do it for money."

"You've got the wrong person," she says, putting on the face of a terrified woman, an innocent woman.

"Save it," I reply. "Here's the skinny. You will not be leaving this little dungeon alive. I watch over my family, including Jasmine. That was your big mistake."

Coldly, the assassin asks, "What do you want, Matthew?"

"Thanks for asking. One question. If your answer pleases me, you'll die the same way Allen Smith died. If you refuse to answer correctly, my good friend will start taking your beautiful face apart like it's a Mr. Potato Head. First, he'll remove your teeth, one by one, with a pair of pliers. Then he'll remove your ears and cute little nose with a straightedge razor, exactly like the ones found in barbershops. I'm sure you can appreciate the irony. In the end, he'll give you a peek in the mirror just to mess with your mind."

"Are you trying to scare me, detective?"

"Absolutely not. But I've watched you enough to know vanity is your weakness. We all like to think we're pretty tough customers until, of course, we find ourselves strapped to a chair in a basement. It kind of puts things in perspective, if you know what I mean."

"We can't cut a deal?"

"Probably not, but what'd you have in mind?"

"Money."

"Oh," I reply. "How much?"

"Eight figures."

"Hot damn! Truth is, there's nothing you have that I want, with the exception of your life. And that's about to end."

Calmly, the assassin says, "There are powerful people looking for me as we speak. I assure you they are not stupid. They will put two and two together, then come for you and your family. They will be ruthless."

"That comment doesn't surprise me in the least. I also think it's straight-up bullshit. Enough with the chitchat. Here's my question. Who hired you to kill Allen Smith?"

"You already know the answer to that question."

"I'm pretty sure I do. But I'd like confirmation."

"Fuck you, detective."

"No. Fuck you, pretty lady." As I begin to walk away, the assassin utters her client's name. I stop and give a thumbs up.

Pop-pop!

154

THIRTY-EIGHT

MATTY

I answer my cell phone. "What's up, Cuz?

"Nothing much and a whole lot at the same time. Can we meet up?" asks Jasmine.

"Of course. Name the time and place."

"The café on 18th Street. Say, around three?"

"I'll see you then." I click off as I walk into The Hall. After spotting Jack at the bar, I wave and take a seat at a distant table where no one can overhear us. Within minutes, Jack makes his way over to the table. Filling two glasses with my favorite water and pushing a glass in my direction, Jack opens with, "What's up?"

"I need a favor."

"Shoot," says Jack. Followed by, "No pun intended."

Ignoring the pun, I say, "I need you to set up a meeting between me and Rosenbaum. At his place. Maybe throw in a bottle of that peaty Scotch."

"When?"

"In the next day or two. Preferably at night, around nine or ten."

"Consider it done. I'll call you when it's official."

"Appreciate it," I say, before downing the glass of water, standing up and leaving.

As soon as I settle in, Jasmine asks, "Who is she?"

Taking a sip from an awaiting double espresso, I pause, then reply, "Not sure, exactly."

"So, you knew about her?"

"I did."

"Do I have anything to worry about?"

"Not anymore."

"Tell me this," says Jasmine, slightly hesitating. "Was she a bad person?"

I study her face before answering. "I didn't know her like you knew her, but let's just say she had some bad qualities. For starters, she killed Allen Smith. And if she would've been allowed to finish what she started, you and I wouldn't be having a conversation right now. Instead, I'd be talking to your ghost."

With a look of concern on her face, Jasmine says, "Then I'll let it go, like it never happened."

"That's good advice all around."

We sit there in silence until my phone rings. I pick it up in the middle of the second ring.

"Yeah."

"It's all set up," says Jack.

"When and where?"

"His place tomorrow night at ten. He'll be waiting for you with a bottle of Scotch.

"Thanks," I say, before ringing off.

THIRTY-NINE

MATTY

Asleep, reclined, an empty whiskey glass sitting on a nearby table—that's the basic view of the future crime scene. Neil Stanza, snoring, is about to stop doing that. Mrs. Stanza, in bed with a TV blaring in the distance, is in a semi-conscious diazepam/cranberry-vodka haze.

My associate had already entered the house, already checked on its occupants, already let me know that all was ready for the ending of another wasted life. Silently walking into the house, small caliber weapon at the ready, I approach the man in the sweat-stained recliner. Without hesitation, I fire two rounds into the crown of Stanza's head.

In her current state, I doubt Mrs. Stanza heard a thing. I'm guessing that's what she'll say when questioned by the police. The cop rumor mill has always echoed a consistent theme: the Stanza union is vacant of any form of marital bliss, and Mrs. Stanza despises Mr. Stanza about as much as he despises her. Or should I say, used to despise her.

I'm dropped off outside *The City Wrap* building by a

trusted associate. Up to Rosenbaum's place I go, feeling like my plan might have a chance at success, yet knowing full well that God laughs at men with plans. Out into the lobby and approaching the front door, I rap a quick double-knock before turning the handle and entering the apartment.

As the door opens, I hear liquid pouring into a glass. I follow the noise. Rosy looks up just as I appear, asking, "What can I do for you, Mr. Marshall?"

"Just take care of your side of a future agreed-upon bargain," I say before sitting down.

"And what would my side of this hypothetical bargain look like?"

"Take care of David O'Shea when the time is right and write a favorable article about me if and when I rise to a more powerful position in this glorious city."

Rosenbaum plays along. "My illustrious paper would have no problem supporting a changing of the guard at certain ranks within this city, a change that favors youth and diversity. Nor would I have a problem, as you say, taking care of David O'Shea. However, that does depend on what you mean exactly when you say 'taking care of' because that could mean a variety of things. Let us not forget that this man you speak of surrounds himself with some scary and committed people."

I lean in toward Rosenbaum, take a sip of Scotch, and pause while savoring its unique taste, then say, "I think I've already taken care of two of those scary problems."

Rosenbaum's raises his eyebrows. "Do tell."

"First, a woman killed Allen Smith. A hired killer employed by David O'Shea. She is no longer with us. I know this because I spoke with her just before she checked out. Don't ask me who she was, because I can guarantee you that even O'Shea doesn't know the answer to that question. Second, O'Shea's old and trusted bodyguard/killer/associate or whatever you want to call him, Neil Stanza, is also permanently out of the picture. Please help me out with this one, though, by keeping his demise on the temporary downlow. No one knows about it except for three people, and two of those people are sitting in this room. I don't want to be the guy who interferes in your business, but you might want to get a reporter outside the Stanza house once 911 is called, probably early tomorrow morning. Believe it or not, he died the same way Smith died: two shots to the head. If you ask me, the police might have a serial killer on their hands. Any questions?"

Rosenbaum remains silent, taking in the unexpected news, before saying, "And what would you like me to do about O'Shea?"

"Before we talk about the assistant chief, or—if you believe the newest word on the street—the soon-to-be chief if he gets his way, let's play a game of I share, you share. I've already told you a few things I know you didn't know, so, your turn."

"Fair enough, but O'Shea positioning himself to be chief with the future mayor is not news to me. Fact is, it's the only career advancement opportunity he has left. Smith had connections who'd hinted as much, and shortly before he died, he told me about it. Apparently, O'Shea is owed some pretty big favors by some powerful folks. They will have to be huge favors for him to dig himself out of the deepest hole he's ever been in. Since you've been extremely up front with me, let me share some information with you. Hopefully, I can toss a couple of nuggets your way."

FORTY

MATTY

Ringtone after ringtone after annoying ringtone. I finally glance down at the number. Not until alerted to a pending message do I check to see what the assistant chief wants. Listening to the curt message, I internally laugh when he uses the word *urgent*, choosing instead to ignore his instructions. I don't need the assistant chief as much as he needs me. Delete. Three hours later a call chimes in again—same number, same ringtone. Time to answer.

"This is Matty."

"Did you get my message?" asks David O'Shea.

"I did."

"You don't return your superior's calls?"

"I don't consider you a superior. What do you want?"

"We need to talk."

Expecting this response, I take control of the conversation by saying, "Meet me tonight at eleven at the address listed inside the envelope on your desk."

Taken by surprise, O'Shea asks, "What envelope?"

"The one with PHP written on it. It's setting on top of your calendar."

There's a pause. I hear paper tearing as I wait.

"You want *me* to come see *you*?" asks O'Shea, insult permeating his tone.

"It's real simple, David. Either you come see me tonight at that address or we don't meet. End of story."

There's another pause. "I'll think about it."

"Think all you want," I say. "But if you're not there at eleven tonight, by yourself, without a gun or wearing a wire, because you will be thoroughly searched, then absolutely all bets are off, as far as we're concerned. Anything goes. Every man for himself. Kind of like the Wild West."

"If I come, I'll have a driver with me."

"No problem, as long as the driver stays inside the car. Tell whoever it is that drives you around these days to empty their bladder before arriving, because if anyone exits that car aside from you, they won't be getting back in. At least not alive. Understood?"

"I hope you know what you're doing. I hope you know exactly what you're getting yourself into, Lieutenant."

"No need to be concerned about my wellbeing, Chief. Let's face it, neither one of us gives a shit about the other, and that's exactly why we should be able to work through our issues without a hitch. See you tonight."

I hit *end*.

FORTY-ONE

DAVID O'SHEA

Moving at a crawl, my driver maneuvers the city vehicle onto the dark streets of the Potrero Hill projects, into a compound of sorts. I'm at a distinct disadvantage, but it's not the first time I've been in this position. If need be, I can be crafty, having dealt with my fair share of scheming politicians, criminals, and fellow cops who thought they could get one over on me.

After easing into curbside parking, my driver kills the engine. I'm early, so I wait, listening to the engine crackle, contemplating my next move. When it's time, I open the rear passenger door and get out. Standing on broken sidewalk, I look around, taking in the dismal scenery before walking over to the first step leading to the meeting spot.

Just prior to ascending, I make out a dark figure standing tall, a shotgun angled across his chest. As my eyes adjust in limited light, I look around some more. Similar figures are spread throughout the apartment grounds. I take a step up.

As I reach the landing, I get the sense that Marshall has employed the services of a ghetto army, their presence felt and observed on each floor, as if ready for battle against many and not just me and an over-matched driver. Two armed men wait for me at the final staircase leading to the third floor. One leads while the other trails; short-barreled shotguns the weapons of choice.

Standing in front of the correctly numbered door, the agreed-upon meeting place, a third man appears. Like kids heading back to class after recess, we troop along in single file around a corner until arriving at another door that can't be seen from the street. A call is made, but no words are spoken. Seconds later, the door opens and I'm ushered inside.

Once inside the apartment, I'm told to strip. I consider protesting, but I'm outnumbered and know that'd be pointless. After a demoralizing search, then getting dressed, I'm led down a long hallway, stopping once we reach a closed door. I'm left unattended as my silent escorts disappear, the last one shutting the lights off as he leaves.

Hearing the front door open, I peer down the hallway and make out a silhouette floating my way. I assume it's Marshall and soon realize I'm correct. As he approaches, he says, "Let's do it in here." He opens the door, brushing by me and entering a barebones environment but for two folding chairs facing each other in the center of the room.

We sit down in the dimly lit room, its only light source coming from a dull, yellow streetlight seeping through a dirty window. Matty speaks first. "What'd you want to meet about?"

"People dying."

"Be a little more specific."

"Stanza," I say. "Why did you kill him?"

"Why did you have Allen Smith killed?"

"I had nothing to do with that."

"Bullshit, David. You see, I spoke with Smith's killer, the one you hired. So, fuck you and your continued lies. But let me be clear, I killed Stanza because he was roaming around elementary schools intimidating little girls. Fuck him. But we're not here to discuss that."

Marshall seems really pissed-off as he stares me down without as much as a blink. It's not an act. Intuitively, I ease my gaze, understanding that reason will be the best way to handle the situation.

Marshall says, "We're here to negotiate my position as assistant chief after Pamela Lee gets elected mayor and appoints you chief. If you don't agree to appoint me to the role, you won't leave this room alive. You won't be getting the easy two-shots-to-the-head treatment, either. It'll be prolonged, relentless pain for you."

"Are you trying to intimidate me, Lieutenant?"

"That's funny, because that's the same question your fine-assed hired killer asked just before she got what was coming to her."

"I've already promised the assistant chief role to someone else."

"Looks like you're going to have to disappoint them. I'll ask you one question before this meeting ends. If your answer is not unequivocally 'yes', then you're about to experience a living hell. It'll turn out better for me if you say 'no.' I'll become chief and no one will be the wiser. Here goes. Will you appoint me to assistant chief after you become chief? Yes or no, motherfucker?"

I'm officially boxed into a corner, at the point of check in a game of chess. My one-word answer: "Yes." Live to face another day.

"Good answer," says Matty. "I was hoping for a no, but I

guess it's not my lucky day. Remember this—if you end up not being a man of your word, you'll end up dead."

I stand up and walk out of the room. This time there's no escort as I fumble down the dark hallway until finally reaching the door. I make my way to an empty street. It's safe to assume I'm still being watched. At last, I spot the city car. I'm relieved it's still there. Once in the back seat, I say, "Let's get out of here." The vehicle's ignition is instantly engaged and the driver speeds away. I now have other concerns on my mind.

FORTY-TWO

MAYOR PAMELA LEE

The voting citizens of San Francisco elected a female mayor: me, Pamela Lee. But the big story isn't one of gender. There have been female mayors before me. The much bigger story is that I'm Chinese, the first Asian mayor in a city with a huge Chinese influence dating back to its racist roots. I'm not a newcomer to San Francisco politics. I may look like a petite librarian—I'm using *that* look to my advantage—but I've been entrenched in the messy venture of city politics since my early twenties, all the while juggling the beginning of a political career with law school. Two decades later, and now in my mid-forties, I've developed deep-seated connections with the right people within the Chinese community, connections that have wisely guided me through a steady uphill battle. I have arrived. The Asian community has arrived. Change is coming.

At first, it took me aback when David O'Shea, the newly appointed chief of police, first approached me to say he'd changed his mind regarding his replacement for the vacated position of assistant chief. His story didn't ring true. Why was he suddenly going with Plan B? A plan I had no prior knowledge of because it didn't exist. But after giving it some thought, after checking into Matthew Marshall's background and having a confidential meeting with Matty, I decided to give my blessing. I see a potential ally in Matty. On top of that, Mr. Marshall is young, black, and good looking. For me, it is the right political move at the right moment in time; a decision that might work to my advantage. Done deal.

I sprinted from the gates talking tough on crime. I also spoke about creating new jobs while bringing more of the world's tourists and their global currency to the fabulous City by the Bay. In truth, I didn't say anything original, but simply touched on rehearsed talking points for the media to gobble up and spew forth. And when major law enforcement matters rear their ugly head, I'll lend a strong voice—along with a sharp video clip with Mr. Marshall by my side. The old days are over. Matty and I are the new look—young professionals of color in powerful positions, giving succinct sound bites in step with repeated political-speak. Away we go, hand in hand.

I doubt David O'Shea gives a rat's ass about the budding relationship between me and the young assistant chief. He's satisfied with his ascension to chief as he grabs tight the brass ring. It looks as if he's come to grips with his prior professional failing, thanks in part to *The City Wrap*. Bottom line: he lacks mayoral pedigree. Those days have long passed him by. He's a dinosaur with, at best, a few more years left in the tank. Let him feel a false sense of importance by running the police department with an iron fist and surrounding himself with loyal lackeys. David O'Shea has been given a gift by the powerful, and he knows it. I'm not concerned about him.

I'm married to a successful attorney with a proper vita.

The counselor, Edward Miller, is bathed in old family money and powerful ties throughout the state. A modern look, big business, and a solid prenup are the keys to our survival as a power couple. It wasn't necessary that I take his last name and we don't spend that much time together except for the occasional charity or business function. Our professional arrangement seems to work for all parties involved, which is a party of many.

Our personal family goals: zero children while maintaining a false facade. The arrangers of our marriage benefit from our continued union. As do we. The topper? We can bed whomever, whenever, because it's an arranged marriage and sleeping with each other is strictly off the table as we both prefer the company of men. The tenets we consistently adhere to and never consider varying from: Keep most aspects of your personal life hidden, and, more importantly, keep your eye on the prize of power and money.

The Hall becomes our late Wednesday night hangout—Matty and me—along with a few city powerbrokers and a half dozen or so trusted media folks thrown in for good measure. No formal invitations are handed out, but if not asked to sit at the big-boy table in the backroom, then you're not welcome. And while the politicians and powerbrokers sip their expensive whiskeys and maintain a certain level of decorum, the media types do not, throwing caution to the wind while getting hammered instead.

I love the food at The Hall, with Mike Gates giving me preferential treatment by preparing an assortment of healthy food options that I can consume in limited quantities while nursing no more than two glasses of white wine the entire evening. Mike Gates refers to me as Madam Mayor and I get a kick out of the Lithuanian chef's stories about the old country.

Jack enjoys his Wednesday night big-table clientele as he watches his mentor, the Professor, navigate in the middle of the throng while drinking like the conservative politician he is not.

One night I asked Jack for a favor, an invitation-only gathering at The Hall to witness a performance by Jasmine. I'd heard about her talents, and now, knowing that she's related to Matty, I wanted to personally see and hear the young musician in the flesh. The political spin for the event will center around raising money for local city artists.

Jack scheduled the performance two weeks out. A member of my staff emailed the invitation list to Jack. This prompted a phone call, asking if it was necessary that his aunt and uncle receive an invitation. I told him, "Not only is it necessary, it's the right thing to do. Like it or not, Jack, you're going to have to deal with them." He didn't jump for joy, but understood my position. I can't ignore the chief entirely.

The media jumped headfirst into my new-mayor hype, even though their early election night projections didn't have me winning. I'm getting great press from all sides of the San Francisco media front. The usually standoffish and wait-and-see *City Wrap* is onboard with me and my proposed staff. They've also given a front-page thumbs-up to the new assistant chief, while the chief, O'Shea, has been relegated to middle-page afterthoughts.

I fully understand that good reviews are a short-term thing. My political success will be judged on getting shit done while managing damage control in a city prone to criticize. If I can't accomplish those two things, the media will turn on me like a pack of hungry jackals. I'm up to the task, having thick skin and, more importantly, big money backing me.

FORTY-THREE

JACK

find myself in a bit of a quandary. I'm falling for an idea, thinking that Jasmine might want what I want . . . commitment. Fat chance!

I'm standing on foreign ground, realizing I'm in a relationship totally out of my control. A rollercoaster of emotions has me feeling uneasy. And as Jasmine prepares to embark on an out-of-state gig—with future gigs lining up— I'm feeling the ugly pangs of jealousy and envy.

Recently, I experienced a dream that still bothers me a great deal. In the dream, I kept Jasmine in a private room within the confines of a guarded castle. I visited her daily to talk and dine and make love. But she couldn't leave. I found the dream akin to a priceless, stolen painting hanging in a secret room for personal viewing only. Imprisoned, wasted art. After waking, I pushed the emotional fog from my brain and murmured, "Damn it, man," as I struggled with possessive thoughts.

Enlightened by my dream, I came to my senses, understanding that I need to back off. Our relationship was never destined for the long haul. Jasmine set early, agreed-upon ground rules, and neither one of us ever raised a flag and called foul. The Professor once told me, "Sometimes with relationships, you need to be comfortable with being uncomfortable."

Even then, I thought, *Easier said than done.*

FORTY-FOUR

ISABELLA

The blade is razor sharp. During training, safety precautions were stressed over and over again. I concentrate hard when handling the knife, understanding a mistake could lead to a nasty cut, followed by blood. My blood. Cutting limes to make Lousy Lime Water is no joke. Slicing one after the other over a prolonged period of time eventually melds into a hazy green. When my mind starts to wander, I know it's time to take a break. With the private event in full swing, I decide to check it out, to see Jasmine perform and to watch the mayor and her posse interact.

I mosey into the main bar during intermission, watching audience members angling toward the bar while others move about and socialize. I see the mayor saddle up to Matty, her hand on his forearm, saying something that makes him laugh and nod in agreement.

Jack seems at ease. He gives me a high-five while passing by, probably because his aunt and uncle are no-shows, even though they had RSVP'd. But his jolly mood soon changes once David O'Shea strides through the front door, alone. Jack isn't the only one who does a double-take. The mayor doesn't hesitate though, approaching David O'Shea and extending a hand as if they're old friends. Looking unsure of himself, Jack heads their way—the odd man out upon arrival. The mayor soon bails, not overdoing a simple greeting while allowing Jack and his uncle some uncomfortable private time. As Jasmine returns to the stage, followed by a young man holding a shiny trumpet, everyone returns to their seats.

They begin, just trumpet and piano. One song down, they shift into another tune, putting the spotlight on the trumpet player, who doesn't seem much older than me. As they finish their final song, the trumpeter bows to the crowd before walking off stage, heading through the back room and out an open door, disappearing into the night as I see the crowd continue to clap.

I hang out for a few more minutes, then head back to the limes. While cutting into a new batch, I sense something. Catching a shadowy blur out of the corner of my eye, I turn to face the prep area entrance—a three-foot opening in a tall cyclone fence. I dry the knife with a bar towel and wait. I don't wait long. He walks up like he belongs, even though he doesn't, standing in the entryway and blocking the only way out. I look up at David O'Shea as he looks down at me from no more than ten feet away. He stands there grinning, creepy-like. I grip the sharp knife and give him my most serious look while angling the tip of the blade in his direction. He mouths something, but my focus is on the game plan, a plan Matty covered with me during one of our "what if" conversations about survival in the city.

Just as David O'Shea takes a step into the prep area, I dart under a long countertop and shuffle as far back as I can go, squatting down while pressing my back into a concrete wall. He'll have to get down on his hands and knees just to see me. I now have the tactical advantage.

Suddenly, another pair of feet appear. I take a peek and see Mike Gates. He's standing inches from the chief of police. Jack walks up behind Mike Gates, looking really pissed off.

Busted, David O'Shea's shoulders slump.

Mike Gates squats down, looks at me, and asks, "You okay?" I shake my head up and down. He extends a hand and I grab hold, duckwalking out from underneath the counter. I keep hold of Mike Gates' hand as he addresses David O'Shea, sternly advising, "You leave now and don't come back ever."

Jack moves to my other side. He looks down at me, sees the knife in my hand, and looks back at his uncle in disbelief.

David O'Shea, wordless, walks away, doing exactly as told.

In a proud moment, I say, "Matty taught me that."

"That Matty is smart fucker of mothers," replies Mike Gates.

I hang out with Jack the remainder of the evening. He won't let me out of his sight. Mike Gates hovers close by. Jack tells me he's in awe that I knew how to protect myself from a bad, bad man. "Time for me to get my shit together," he says, before adding to no one in particular, "He's not gonna stop until he gets what he wants."

As the VIPs file from The Hall—some stumbling, most being driven home—Jack explains the situation to Matty while I stand at his side. Smiling, Matty says, "This here little girl would've cut that chump up if he tried to go after her." To Jack, he says, "You need to take care of that uncle of yours. You understand that, right?"

"I do. Is there a possibility we could get together to discuss a plan of action?"

Matty's reply: "I love the way you white boys talk. Call me tomorrow, Jack." Matty gives me a fist bump and ruffles my hair before following the mayor outside.

FORTY-FIVE

DAVID O'SHEA

I cut to the chase halfway through a vodka martini.

"I need your assistance."

"With what?"

"Taking out Donna O'Shea."

"As in kill her?"

"Is that going to be a problem?" I ask.

"Not a problem. I'm somewhat familiar with her basic day-to-day routines, but I'll need some time to get it down to a gnat's ass."

"As you said, not a problem. No rush. Let's play the long game. We have to get this right, with no mistakes and nothing leading back to me, to us.

"Understood."

"All along, to me anyway, the little girl was the easy mark. Not only was I wrong, but I miscalculated who I was dealing with. I tested the waters last night and, to my surprise—even though I shouldn't have been—she's protected by an entire group of people who hover about like squawking hens. One in particular who will kill for her. Too many eyes. Too risky. Fact is that most folks are overly sensitive when it comes to kids."

"That they are."

"The good thing about Donna is that she's blood. She brought Jack into this world and is as much a confidant to him as the Jew is. But in a different kind of way. In a more personal way. Let's get personal."

"I agree. He'll then understand how much of an arrogant fool he's been and how much he's underestimated the situation he's in."

"Remember, we can't get arrogant and we can't underestimate Jack or the people who surround him. We have to be on the same page."

"We're always on the same page."

"That's what I wanted to hear. So, take your time and check in now and then with updates."

"Of course."

FORTY-SIX

JASMINE

Cruising through a neighborhood in the Outer Richmond, I thank Jack for tagging along. He utters a low-toned, "No problemo, señorita. Ana's covering for me at the club tonight, and thanks for driving by my mom's house. I like keeping tabs on her, especially when she's none the wiser."

We're off to see the talented trumpeter, Nick Barnes, perform at a coffeehouse a block off of Geary. At sixteen, the young musician is becoming well known in jazz circles on the West Coast—San Francisco, Los Angeles, Portland, Seattle, Vancouver. I'd committed to swinging by as a return favor for Nick playing at the mayor's private function.

After parking the car, Jack says, "I didn't know The Blue Bean was still in business. It's been years since I've been here."

"You probably need to get out more. You know, socialize with a few folks outside your circle of four."

As we walk through the doors, a controlled, muted note sails through the air, mesmerizing a packed house eating out of the trumpeter's hand. Standing just inside the coffeehouse entrance, I walk over and hug the owner, Monica Martinez, like we've known each other for years and not just a few weeks. I introduce Jack to Monica right as Nick Barnes finishes a soulful tune. Accompanied by a slap bass, the duo jumps into an upbeat number as the sweat pours, glaring blue lights shining down on glistening faces.

Monica asks Jack if he'd like a cold brew. Jack says sure. Monica and I head for the kitchen, engaged in full-on conversation. The crowd at The Blue Bean is a mixed bag of ethnicities and ages that range from teenagers to mid-twenties, tops. As Jack approaches thirty, I'm sure he's feeling his age, what with being surrounded by a club full of high-energy youngsters.

We return and Monica hands Jack a drink while saying, "Cheers!"

Jack's eyes go from me to Monica and back to me. He knows something's up. Aiming a straw between ready lips, Jack sucks in the dark, cold coffee and appears pleasantly surprised. Cocking an eyebrow in Monica's direction, he says, "I'm very much a cold brew snob and I have to say this is pretty damn good."

"I'm glad you like it," replies Monica. "I stole the recipe from you."

"Really. How'd you do that?"

Monica turns toward me, my cue to confess. "I'll come clean, Jack. Isabella and I met Monica at a street fair. Once we found out she owned a coffeehouse, well, it only made sense that she start making cold brew the right way. Isabella and I came down to The Blue Bean one day and your little protégé schooled Miss Martinez in the art of Jack O'Shea's secret cold brew recipe."

Jack blurts out, "Traitors," way too loud, then laughs. Still curious, he asks Monica, "What brand of coffee is this?"

"It's an extra dark French roast that we get from a family-operated farm in Mexico. We call it La Magia and roast it right here. I was hoping you'd sample some at your place."

Speaking to no one in particular, Jack says, "Why do I feel like I've been set up? Probably because I have." Then he says to Monica, "I'd love to try some. Do you have a fresh batch? The darker the better."

"I was hoping you'd ask," replies Monica. "I have five pounds ready to go in back, freshly roasted. On the house, of course, for nabbing your recipe."

"No problem, and thanks. By the way, I used to hang out here back in the day when I lived out in the avenues. When did you become the owner?"

"I moved here from New York a little over ten years ago. It's where I landed my first job. I started managing the place about two years after that. When the opportunity presented itself, I bought into the business with the original owner, Big Sandy. She's my best friend and mentor."

"I remember Big Sandy. I'm glad you two are making a go of things."

Monica excuses herself, looking at her cell phone while saying, "Duty calls." I give her a hug and Jack shakes her hand. We redirect our focus to Nick Barnes. With accomplished chops, the trumpeter rounds out an eerie note that sounds a lot like a howling wolf.

Listening to the young musician is a treat. During intermission, I introduce Jack to Nick. Jack agrees to set aside some time so he and the young man can meet and agree on a future performance date at The Hall. Once they're done talking, I join Nick on stage and sing an old Etta James hit.

As we head home, I apologize for giving away the cold

brew recipe. Jack tilts his head in my direction, saying, "No apologies necessary." Then he gets serious. "Was I the oldest guy there?"

I poke him in the ribs and tell him he was definitely the oldest dude in the club. Jack says, "Ouch!" before adding, "If you don't mind, let's drive by my mom's house one more time."

FORTY-SEVEN

JACK

Back to the ocean I go. To train. To get into the kind of shape I was in a decade ago. The first week is brutal, the cold water overpowering. But the pace and feel of ocean swimming quickly returns—muscle memory—including the endorphin rush when strenuous exercise becomes routine.

In addition to swimming, I train with Matty three nights a week. Matty trains like a boxer, which means I now train like one, too. Also, the art of knife fighting is introduced at Matty's insistence—a series of simple moves: reach, grab, pull, thrust, stab-stab-stab. Over and over until instinctive—a dancer dancing a familiar dance.

Matty is a calming influence. Getting hit by the quicker and more experienced street fighter also gives me a bit of confidence, a perceived toughness, but not overly so, with Matty making damn sure of that during post-workout discussions regarding mental focus and the proper execution of plans.

After two months of serious training, planning, and

scouting the consistent patterns of our target, I inform Matty I'm ready. He thinks it over for all of a nanosecond before shaking his head no and saying, "One more month." Not flinching, I agree, then stick a well-thrown body shot, a left hook seeking his liver. Seconds later, I pay dearly for my cockiness.

On the work front, I enter into business dealings with Monica Martinez and Big Sandy after sampling their coffee beans. I need to mix things up now and then, letting my regulars decide if change makes sense. If so, go with it. If not, then rely on the sure thing. *Don't become stagnant in business dealings,* is my takeaway.

While meeting with the two coffeehouse owners, I agree to show Monica how to make another one of my cherished recipes—and it's not the Lousy Lime Water. I vow to teach her my version of organic whipped cream. Interested, Monica shows up at The Hall the following day to witness my sweet creation firsthand. When leaving, after thanking me, she says, "I had a good time today, Jack. Maybe I'll return the favor down the road."

"Maybe," I reply.

Jasmine returns from Portland and requests some private time . . . just me and her. By her tone, it feels like we're about to have a serious conversation.

"Jack, let me get right to the point. I've landed the opening act gig for the upcoming Spangled Hash Southwestern Tour. I think it's time we break off our relationship. With me traveling, it won't be fair to either of us."

Having finally put things in perspective regarding our relationship, I welcome her candor. "I couldn't agree more. I get it. You've been up front about our relationship from the get-go."

"I'm sorry, Jack."

"Don't be. I'm happy for you. I mean it. Let's celebrate with some champagne."

"How about something stronger?"

"Bourbon?"

"Much better."

"You know, if you're open to it, we could throw a going-away bash at The Hall. Make it the first show of the tour. You open; Spangled Hash closes."

"I would love that, Jack. Can you make it happen?"

"I'll put it in motion, reach out to Barney Kellogg with Spangled Hash and sort out the details."

"Let's do it. If Barney's in, I'm in."

My thinking was spot on. We end a relationship based on temporary, only temporary. Friends it is. For the first time I can recall, I want to be in a committed relationship. But it won't be with Jasmine.

The following day, back to the ocean, back to the gym, and back to Matty's guidance in the face of future danger.

Spending more time with Isabella since the bullpen incident, I find myself contemplating family. Not my current family but starting one. I choose to entertain these thoughts and not push them away. I razz Isabella for giving away the cold brew recipe. She counters by pointing out that I gave away the whipped cream recipe. In unison, with the tips of our noses nearly touching, we both say, "Not the Lousy Lime Water recipe," before breaking into gut wrenching laughter.

I invite my mother to dinner at The Hall. We dine in the backroom. Mike Gates steals the show with lamb shank stew. My mom comments about my change in appearance. I tell her I've been working out—swimming, boxing.

"It's something other than that, but I can't quite put my

finger on it," she says.

I tell her to take it easy on the wine. She brushes aside my sarcasm. I've arranged for a limo service to take her home, ignoring her fuss that it's a waste of money. Also, the driver—per my earlier instructions—will remain outside her house until she's safely tucked away inside. After that, he'll park down the street and keep watch for an additional hour.

Within minutes after my mother's departure, my phone buzzes. It's Monica Martinez. I answer the call.

FORTY-EIGHT

JACK

The bash at The Hall is a blast. Friends, family, and fans show up in abundance. Other local musicians join in the frivolity, their respective talents on display as they join Jasmine and Spangled Hash on stage. Petty city ordinances are ignored, and no one seems to mind.

The following morning a pack of drunken musicians stumble from the bar into harsh sunlight, taking one final toke before piling onto tour buses heading for the southwest. Well-wishers wave goodbye.

Returning inside, I look at Ana and she looks at me. We both shake our heads as we ready the club for another day's business.

"You going to be all right?" asks Ana, as she walks toward the kitchen.

"In time," I reply.

"I still love you."

"I love you, too."

I leave work as soon as the lunch crowd wanes. I stop at home and grab my gear before driving to the beach. After an hour in the ocean, I check my phone and see that I have two messages: one from Matty, one from Jasmine. Jasmine slurs a barely audible goodbye while band members whoop it up in the background. Matty's message is brief, "Go time tomorrow night. Get some rest."

I head home for much needed sleep.

That evening, I meet with Matty for our usual training session. We don't train. Instead, we meticulously go over plans.

The following night, I'll enter the ocean from a select location while my uncle walks along the beach. David O'Shea is predictable: Monday through Friday same time, same place. Roughly fifteen minutes later, I'll exit the ocean and make my approach. After recognizing me, likely wondering why I was in the ocean, I'll mention that I'm out for a late-night swim. Not a bizarre response, because his son and I used to do it on the regular. Once in handshaking distance, and without hesitation, I'll latch onto one of his arms and pull him forward while thrusting a thin, sharp knife into him, just below his sternum, burying the blade handle deep. Pulling the knife out, I'll immediately puncture his carotid artery—jab, jab, jab— and then retreat back to the safe confines of chilly saltwater, swimming away as he bleeds out.

If O'Shea's new bodyguard happens to see a dark figure appear from the ocean and approach his boss, it won't matter in the least because of distance and terrain. By the time he figures anything out, if he figures it out, it'll be too late. I'll be doing the backstroke as his boss breathes his last breath.

Surprisingly, I get a good night's sleep and feel on top of my game as I walk to work. Leaving The Hall after lunch rush, I return home to rest and engage in mental preparation.

Matty stops by at suppertime, not to eat but to talk. We go

over the plan one final time, minute detail by minute detail. Matty won't be there when it goes down. He'll be at a political function with the mayor. I'll be flying solo. Right as Matty leaves, he tosses a set of keys in my direction while saying, "Don't fuck up." His way of showing confidence in me.

It's time. I load my gear into the provided stripped-down car and drive to Ocean Beach. Parking a block off the main road and across the street from sand dunes, I squeeze into a wetsuit and make damn sure I have everything I need. The car will not be there when I get back. I place the backpack containing my clothes on the passenger-side floorboard while placing the keys under the driver's seat. I exit the vehicle and gently shut the door before walking across the highway into the darkness of the dunes.

After a seventy-yard trek, I arrive at the water's edge. Walking into the ocean, I reach chest-high water before going under. It will be an easy swim, the ocean calm, lake-like. I make it out to the target point, stop and tread water while turning and facing shore. After gathering my wits, I swim toward land. Assisted by the push of a small wave and sensing shallow water, I extend my legs until my feet touch sand. I perform a slow breaststroke, finally stopping once my knees scrape bottom. Removing the knife from its sheath with my right hand, I assume a crouched stance and cautiously step from the ocean.

Looking to my left, then my right, and finally toward the parking lot, it becomes obvious I'm alone. The chief is nowhere to be found. We've accounted for this: Murphy's Law. I kneel and wait the planned five minutes. Just to make sure, I wait another five. Nothing changes. I'm disappointed but relieved.

Turning around, I go back into the ocean and swim the reverse course from earlier. I hike back through the dunes and over to where I'd parked the car. In its place is a white panel van. I knock twice on the back door and it opens. I climb into the pitch-black interior, paying little attention to who's inside. Instead, I search for a bench seat. After finding it, I park my wet ass.

I feel for my backpack under the seat and quickly find that, too. After removing the wetsuit, I towel off before getting dressed. I stuff the wetsuit and knife and towel inside the backpack.

A while later, the van pulls into an alley a few blocks from The Hall. I get out the same way I got in. I stroll to the club as if stopping by for a nightcap.

Mike Gates calls out the second I walk in, "You like whiskey shot, boss man?"

To which I reply, "Make it a double."

"Then we drink together," says the Lithuanian chef.

FORTY-NINE

JACK

Rapid-fire knocking wakes me from a light sleep. Getting out of bed and donning a robe, I yell, "Who is it?"

There's a return shout from the lobby. "Rosy and Matty."

I open the door, saying, "What's up?" Both men charge by, settling near a stereo speaker.

Matty says, "What happened last night? I never heard from you."

"I stuck to the plan: 'If nothing happens, don't bother calling.'"

"You're telling me nothing happened?"

"Well, not exactly. I was there, knife in hand. But my uncle never showed."

Rosenbaum looks at Matty, then back at me, finally saying, "That was your plan? I'm glad he didn't show up. A lot of shit could've gone wrong."

Matty, suddenly annoyed, says, "It would've worked if the motherfucker would've been there like he was supposed to be. But thanks for your input, Mr. Pessimist. So, where is he then, Jack?"

I mimic Rosenbaum, looking from one to the other before asking, "What do you mean, where is he? How would I know?"

Matty, finally realizing I'm out of touch, glances at his watch and says, "Your uncle's missing. Your aunt made a call to the department a little over an hour ago. Nobody knows where he's at."

"Really? Maybe he's somewhere getting hammered. That kind of behavior runs in our family."

"We kicked that around," replies Matty. "But there's a huge problem with that scenario. His new driver, Nick Jansen, was found dead a mile from Ocean Beach in an unmarked city car. Another bullet-to-the-head dead guy. No trace of your uncle, with the exception of his cell phone, which was found underneath Nick."

"That doesn't sound good," I say.

"No shit," says Matty.

"I second that," adds Rosenbaum. "So let me get this straight. You planned to kill O'Shea, but he didn't show up because someone beat you to the punch or he skipped town. Is that what you're telling me?"

"Sounds about right," I reply.

"Wow," says Rosenbaum. "All right then. Jack, make yourself available in case we need to talk. Matty, what are you going to do?"

"I have to get with the investigative team to see where they're at with this. After that, I'll fill the mayor in, no pun intended."

"If anyone needs me, you know the drill," says Rosenbaum. "I'll get back to you in no time. Reach out if you hear anything. Jack, do you think you should stop by your aunt's house and see how she's doing?"

"No. And why would you, of all people, ask me that?"

Rosenbaum doesn't respond, deciding to leave sensitive family matters alone.

As they start to walk out the door, I say, "Pretty weird shit, right?"

They leave me hanging as they both ignore my brilliant observation.

194

FIFTY

MATTY

After meeting with the investigative team, I walk into the mayor's office for a private sit-down. The situation at hand reeks of potential bad press for the police department. An illegal slush fund has been uncovered; the money controlled by David O'Shea and him alone. The account information was found in the top drawer of the chief's desk. Pretty convenient. I explain this to the mayor and right away she asks, "How much money are we talking about?"

"Over six-hundred-thousand dollars as of yesterday. Closer to seven."

"And today?"

"Zilch. The entire amount has been withdrawn. It was transferred to another account but only stayed in that account for a short while, then it was off and running until it vanished. The financial guys are at a loss as to where it went."

"Do you think he skipped town? Or do you think he's dead?"

"My gut tells me he's dead, but I could be wrong. That said, it feels like dead to me."

"So, what should I tell the media? By the way, you look very good in black."

"Thank you for the compliment. You should try it on for size sometime. Back to the media thing. I'd get your staff preparing something right away that sounds like you're concerned about the chief. Conveniently mention that a private slush fund was uncovered connected to the chief and not the department and it appears as if it's been drained of all funds. Let them know you're on top of it, that a thorough investigation is underway by trusted, competent personnel—with the chief's safety being your utmost concern."

"Sounds real close to what I was thinking. Especially the part about me being on top of it. So, do you want to be chief?"

"I do."

"I'll see what I can do about that," replies the mayor. "Keep me updated if anything new pops up."

"You know I will." I grin at the mayor's final comment. With a busy day ahead, I exit the sex-charged office before things get out of hand.

I make my way over to *The City Wrap* building and up to Rosenbaum's apartment. Once pleasantries are exchanged and we're seated, Rosenbaum says, "I apologize for my comment this morning about your plan not having a chance at success."

"Not to worry, my wise friend. But I do appreciate you clearing the air on that one small slight. With that out of the way, what do you think went down?"

Rosenbaum scooches forward and asks, "Was it difficult finding the connection between the chief and the alleged secret account?"

I tilt my head, inwardly impressed that Rosenbaum has

knowledge of confidential information that's off-limits to the press. "Neither you, nor any member of the media for that matter, should know about a secret account. But since we're talking off the record, I'll say this to you and only you: It was extremely easy to find the connection between O'Shea and the illegal slush fund. An imbecile could have found it and put two and two together."

"All departments have leaks, my future chief. And, with what you've just told me being held in the strictest of confidence, I'd have to say our former chief is dead. I'd bet my life on it."

"I agree with you, Rosy. I'm 99.9% sure of it."

FIFTY-ONE

JACK

Back at The Hall, me, Ana, and Mike Gates kick around the whereabouts of—and ideas of what happened to—David O'Shea. Ana says, "Do you think he has a young squeeze on the side down in South America or something?"

"I would go to Tahiti like American actor Brando, no?" says Mike Gates.

"I honestly think he's dead," I reply.

"Why is that?" asks Ana.

"Because his bodyguard is dead and his cell phone was left behind. I know it looks like the opposite of that, as if the dude skipped town. But that's too obvious. It looks that way because that's exactly what didn't happen, you know what I mean?"

Mike Gates chimes in with, "I was lost once you say obvious."

Ana adds, "This is too much. What new dose of crazy is going to happen next in this city?"

"You guys want a shot of booze from a five-hundred-dollar bottle of tequila that I have locked up under the bar and haven't told either one of you about?" I ask.

Ana pipes in, "It's still morning, Jack."

To which Mike Gates says, "It is evening in homeland."

I take out a set of keys, kneel, and unlock a cabinet underneath the bar. Seconds later I produce a clear bottle with a handwritten label.

Somewhere in Lithuania someone smiles, as we each down a shot of smooth, blanco tequila.

Jack called his mom and told her the news. She said she'd call Maddie O'Shea.

Within the hour, she called back and said she couldn't get through until Maddie determined she wasn't some weirdo or the media or both.

"She rushed me off the phone. You'd think knowing each other for over forty years would mean something. I guess not."

"Aunt Maddie was always kind of cold, Mom."

"The fact is, son, Maddie O'Shea is ice-cold and getting colder."

Matty barely clears the front door at The Hall when Mike Gates yells, "You like shot of best tequila ever?"

"As long as you serve it with some of that water."

Mike Gates pours a shot for me, Matty, and himself.

Ana says," That's it until cocktail hour."

I load two shots of the good stuff, water glasses, and a bottle of Lousy Lime Water onto a tray and take it over to an empty table.

Sitting down, Matty and I now have time to discuss my prior night's escapades. I fill him in on the personal details: the way I felt at each stage along the way while executing the plan, wanting to shit myself as soon as I came out of the ocean, knowing full well what lay ahead. I thank Matty for the training and planning and for having the faith in me to deliver.

"Not a big deal, my Caucasian comrade," replies Matty after I finish my awkward thank you. We toast, clinking shot glasses before downing the expensive booze. We sit in silence, both nursing a large glass of water. Soon thereafter, Matty gets up to leave, saying, "Let's keep training three nights a week. I needed that. I still need it. Thanks for getting me out of a rut and my soft ways."

"Sure thing."

The front runner to be the next chief of police of San Francisco, the man with balls the size of Idaho potatoes, strolls from The Hall with a pronounced swagger.

Hundreds of miles off the ever-stretching coastline of the Americas, a small freighter cruises toward Osaka, Japan. On board—asleep in a private cabin four decks below—is David O'Shea. The nondescript ship is in no hurry to reach its destination port.

FIFTY-TWO

JASMINE

Coming to their feet and cheering, the crowd at The Whiskey Barn in downtown Albuquerque has just been treated to a kick-ass, three-hour performance—my act, followed by Spangled Hash, followed by a combination of the two. For me it's a coming home. After a huge hug from my biggest fan, my mom says, "Girl from the rez done good."

Barney Kellogg takes a liking to me. "I dig your work ethic, kid. Your attention to detail."

He passes along tricks of the trade and subtle advice so my vocal cords can survive the abuse of touring. Sponge-like, I heed his wise words, coming to the quick conclusion that playing in the city and sleeping in my own bed is easy-peasy compared to playing at different venues while dealing with the confines of a bus night in and night out.

"Thanks for the advice, old man."

He grins and shakes his head as we wrap up another show.

Before leaving Albuquerque and heading to Santa Fe, my mom cooks a feast for the entire crew. Better yet, she brings the food to us. We wolf it down with very little talking, thankful to be eating a homecooked meal and not takeout.

Finally, back on the bus and on the road, traveling, traveling, traveling. Wanderers have it in their blood, and it helps to be a wanderer when your chosen profession is that of a touring musician.

In Santa Fe I meet an artist by the name of Rachel Mann. She's my age with nothing to hide, the antithesis of my lover in San Francisco. With months gone by, I can barely remember that certain someone's name, if name told was true. Rachel's different: younger, thicker, funnier. She also has strong, workman-like hands—the hands of a sculptor.

We're barely a half hour into getting to know each other when she invites me to her place, saying, "You want to check out my loft?"

"Sure," I reply.

The Santa Fe stop is a ten-day stayover: Thursday night, Friday night, weekend night gigs. Monday and Tuesday are our off days, with band rehearsal falling on Wednesday. This gives me and Raquel plenty of time to get to know each other.

I end up spending most of my time with Rachel during the Santa Fe stop. Compared to the bus or a ratty motel room her loft seems like a mansion. It's also a working studio, with Rachel creating art at ground level as natural light oozes through heavily tinted roll-up doors. Concrete all-round, red-iron support beams brace the walls; at their height bending inside the overhead. The two-level structure screams of open space. Situated atop a massive steel staircase is Rachel's welcoming bed—centered on a pallet platform. For nine straight days we explore.

With our time up, we vow to stay in touch. The young sculptor can't wait to come to California, to San Francisco—a city she's never been to. I want to show her the city and need to get my own place to do it properly.

When the bus leaves Santa Fe the tour is halfway over, as we head south then east into Barney Kellogg's old stomping grounds of West Texas. *The cool thing about traveling with musicians, I think, is that we make an effort to respect each other's lives while coping in close confines. So much different than dealing with the hyenas out in the real world.*

As I lounge inside the bus—mesmerized by motion and humming tires and thoughts of Rachel—my eyes settle on an article in a West Coast newspaper. The piece mentions the missing chief, missing money, and poses the question, "Did he skip town or is he dead?"

FIFTY-THREE

JACK

In the grips of a semi-global media frenzy, San Francisco is spotlighted nationally—with foreign media types flying in to exploit the chaotic situation as well. It's not every day that a major city's chief of police turns up missing along with $687K lifted from a private bank account that apparently nobody else knew about. Pamela Lee is getting her fair share of camera time, the new mayor shamelessly taking full advantage of the media circus like any politician would. Matty has been appointed interim chief of police and is personally overseeing the investigative team assigned to the bizarre case. As far as the investigation is concerned, there really isn't much going on because my uncle appears to be long gone without a trace.

My mom tells me that my aunt is holding up—old school, stoically—hunkering down in the privacy and protection of her home. Daily, when leaving the house at seven twenty-five for church, she's escorted by two patrolmen while hordes of media types wielding cameras and handheld devices shout out ridiculous questions and comments and insults, displaying modern-day newsgathering at its worst. Once Mass is over, a repeat performance is played out on the return trip. She doesn't dare leave the house to go shopping for basic necessities, but instead sends an errand boy. The so-called journalists swarm, wanting to know what's in the shopping bag. Two percent milk or whole? Double or single ply tissue? On and on it goes until it becomes back page news after someone famous for being famous takes over the spotlight by craftily arranging a media push surrounding the accidental-on-purpose timely release of their personal sex tape.

A week before the traveling musicians return to San Francisco for a tour-ending show at The Hall, I find myself in the company of Monica Martinez on a regular basis. Six days prior to their final show, Monica and I end up in a serious lip lock at the Blue Bean—so engrossed in the kiss that we lose our balance and stumble into a coffee roaster. Five days before the anticipated return of the haggard performers, I wind up in a naked wrestling match at my place with the passionate coffeehouse owner. Days four, three, and two prior to their return, I wake up next to the warm-bodied native New Yorker and find it rather comforting. One day before their scheduled return, Monica Martinez and I are an official item—secure in our newfound, committed relationship.

The touring band's return to San Francisco is anticlimactic. They cancel their final show at The Hall after two members come down with the flu. Jasmine chills at her aunt's house, recovering from the effects of being on the road.

One gloomy morning Jasmine meets me at The Hall for coffee and a round of catch up. She eventually mentions Rachel while I speak of Monica. With that out of the way, tensions wither, both content with the other's good fortune.

But not overly so. Jasmine wants to know why no one called when the chief went missing. I tell her that Matty said to leave it be while she was on the road. Jasmine rolls her eyes and says, "Protective men, huh? You didn't think I was going to hear about that? I wasn't on Mars, Jack." I tell her to take it up with Matty. Jasmine, bruised by my indifference, gives me a listless hug before taking off to go see friends.

While sitting at the bar nursing a cold brew, I hear the front door open. With my back to the door, I look into the bar's paneled mirror and watch in disbelief as Maddie O'Shea strides toward me in a tight-fitting business suit. I'm caught off guard, having not seen or spoken to her in a long time. She sashays up to the bar, takes a seat next to me, and says, "Fix me a drink, Jack."

"Sure, Aunt Maddie. What would you like?"

"Bourbon, neat."

As I walk behind the bar, I look over at Mike Gates, who's sitting at a table studying a prearranged chess problem and acting as if he didn't notice Maddie O'Shea prance up to the bar. Nobody with a pulse could've missed that.

I pour a favorable amount of Kentucky bourbon into a tumbler and place it in front of her. "It's been a while," I say.

Picking up the tumbler, she says, "It has." She downs the bourbon before saying, "Now give your auntie a kiss," and she leans over the bar. Feeling weird, I cautiously lean forward as Maddie moves in as if to kiss my right cheek, but instead extends farther so her painted lips hover on the fringe of my ear. Without warning, she whispers, "I want Sean's suicide note," then crosses the line and flicks the tip of her tongue inside my ear.

Shocked, I yell, "What the fuck?" while jerking my head back and shooting a look of disgust in her direction.

Unfazed, she nonchalantly says, "One more please," as she pushes the empty glass my way.

After refilling her drink, I grab the nearest bar rag and wipe saliva from my ear. I watch as she slams her second drink. "How much do I owe you?" she asks, opening her tiny purse resting on the bar.

"It's on the house." I reply, before sarcastically adding, "By the way, it's not a note. It's a letter. A detailed letter."

"I thought for sure you were going to say, 'What note?' or 'I don't know what you're talking about.' Smart move coming clean, Jack, because I followed you down to the ocean that night. So, understand this: I don't give two fucks what you call it, I just want the bloody thing," yells Maddie O'Shea, no longer concerned about being discreet.

I try my darndest to act unfazed by her startling news. "Well, I don't have it handy, if that's what you were thinking. It's not like I keep it in my back pocket."

"Wherever it is, I want it. David wanted it, but he's gone. So now it falls on me."

"I'll have to give it some thought, Maddie. A lot of thought. But remember this, it was left for me; not for you or your husband."

"I don't care who it was left for, Jack. So, when can I expect a decision?"

"Give me a month."

"A month it is. To the day. You call me. And if you don't, I'll be back and I'll make a scene. So, be a man of your word." With that, she spins a one-eighty and hops off the barstool while clutching her purse. Her dismount is smooth, but then she stalls—adjusting her snug skirt—before continuing on in four-inch pumps. Maddie O'Shea walks out of The Hall in a hip-swaying straight line.

Stunned, I say to no one in particular, "What the fuck was that?"

To which Mike Gates, peering up from the chessboard, says, "What the fuck is right, boss. You have scary family member there."

Mike Gates stands up and heads for the bar. After removing a bottle of Russian Vodka from the cooler, he says, "Join me, comrade?"

"Yeah," I say. "Let's do a six-shooter."

"Six-shooter, yes. Like American cowboy, no?"

FIFTY-FOUR

JACK

The day after my aunt's browbeating, I cross the lobby and rap successive double knocks on Rosenbaum's door. Expecting me, he shouts, "Come in." Once again sitting and facing each other, I lay out my prior day run-in with the odd-acting Maddie O'Shea. I cover all bases, leaving nothing out: her walking into The Hall unexpectedly; her formfitting outfit; her saddling up to the bar; her ordering bourbon for breakfast; the whisper followed by a repugnant tongue-flicking kiss; her getting louder after I became sarcastic; her demand; her threat; her second drink; her surprising comment about following me to the ocean long ago; and her dismount from the stool before sashaying out of the bar.

"What do you think, Professor?"

"I think we are no longer speculating, because we now know for sure what your uncle wanted." Rosy looks up at the ceiling, composing himself before looking back at me.

"The proverbial ball is in your court, Jack. The letter was left for you, not for her, not for him. If you want to give it up, that's your call. Holding onto it won't do you any good at this point as long as the chief is no longer with us—and I'm betting he's not.

"That sounds about right," I say.

"But her threatening you with the possibility of causing a future scene is bullshit. Jesus, Jack, we could print your cousin's letter in the paper if we wanted to. We have the original, not some hokey copy. Talk about a scene and piling more shit onto the not-so-nice memory of David O'Shea. So, screw her. If you decide to give it to her, do it on your terms. When you feel like it. Or shred the damn thing."

"We're on the same page, Professor. I'm leaning toward giving it to her. But I'll do it when it feels right, on my terms just like you said and not a second sooner. I'll give her a call and let her know how it's gonna shake out. If she chooses to mess with me, I'll shred it. You're right, screw her."

"Anything else, Jack? I only ask because I haven't eaten yet and I'm starving and craving sweets."

"No, that was it. We're done."

"Good. You want a cup of coffee and a piece of cake?"

"Sure, let's get our caffeine and sugar on."

After coffee and cake, I head back to my place and make the call.

"Hello."

"It's Jack."

"And?"

"I'll give you the letter when the time is right."

"When will the time be right?"

"Not sure, Maddie. I'm going to share it with a couple of people first. When I'm ready, I'll find you. Not a second before."

"I see. So, it's Maddie now. No more Auntie."

"We're not blood related. Never were. I always saw through the fake family bullshit. So, don't threaten me by telling me you're going to make a scene. If you want a scene, I'll make a bigger one by having Sean's letter printed in *The City Wrap*. Rosenbaum already said he'd do it. Go away, Maddie. Mind your own business. You'll get the letter when I decide you get the letter."

There's a long pause. For some odd reason, I think about her tongue. Finally, her calm response, "Fuck you, Jack."

With the letter in tow, I make two more stops. First, I sit at a familiar kitchen table out in the avenues, a table where I used to eat cereal before trotting off to school. I wait while my mother reads the letter. When she finishes, she gets up and vomits in the sink. I apologize and she waves me off. Composing herself, she asks, "You've held on to this the entire time?"

At first I assume she's referring to the letter. I'm wrong. What she's really talking about are my thoughts and holding on to those bad thoughts for over a decade. After clarification, I answer honestly, acknowledging that I've held on to a terrible secret for quite some time. She approaches and gives me a hug. Crying, she says, "Things were much different than I imagined them to be."

My next stop is downtown. I find myself sitting across from Matty at an oversized desk. Matty reads the letter. He doesn't puke and he doesn't embrace me. He simply says, "That's some fucked up shit."

I'd come to the same conclusion long ago. Matty says he'll see me at The Hall later that evening for a high-octane nightcap.

FIFTY-FIVE

JACK

The day has arrived. Monica moves in with me as Jasmine moves into Monica's old apartment. Monica and I have crossed over to a serious relationship while Jasmine gets her own place, her own space—and just in time with Rachel arriving in a week and a day. The transition is seamless, with Monica leaving behind a bed, a dinette set, and a sofa and ottoman as much needed housewarming gifts—only taking select clothes and a few personal items. Jasmine walks into a plug-and-play apartment and the landlord doesn't raise the rent because he's handed the gift of optimum occupancy.

I dig my new roommate, lover, partner. Monica seems fond of me as well. One evening as I come home from work, I walk into candlelight and a home-cooked meal. Caught off guard, I say to Monica, "What's the occasion? Please don't tell me I missed an anniversary: our first kiss or that time you stole my cold brew recipe."

"Just dinner for my man. Have a seat, big boy."

Hearty pork chops, garlic mashed potatoes, steamed green beans, and a glass of white wine are on the menu. We dive in, exchanging idle chitchat. After finishing, I say, "That was awesome."

"Just something I threw together last minute," teases Monica, while we clear the table and wash dishes. As we retire to the new couch, Monica says, "Jack, I'm crazy scared and crazy happy."

"Yeah, what's going on, babe?"

"To be blunt, Jack, you and I are going to have a baby."

I turn and face her. "Honey, those are the best words I've ever heard." We embrace and kiss.

Afterward, I call my mom, and then Monica gets on the phone with the only living grandparent of the baby to be. Later, I call Rosenbaum, who politely hangs up after hearing the word "baby." Before I know it, there's a knock on the door. I open it to find Rosenbaum lifting a bottle in the air while saying, "Let's celebrate!" All three of us have a group hug/cry/laugh.

After the Professor leaves, I make my final call of the evening—to Matty. I share the news with the newly appointed chief, asking my old friend if he'll perform our wedding ceremony.

Matty asks, "When and where?"

"In roughly a month at The Hall."

Matty says, "Deal."

I give Monica a thumbs up.

She says, "We need rings."

"I'll get those," I say as I thank Matty and hang up. Off to bed we go.

With my head resting on a pillow, I say, "I take it Big Sandy already knows."

"She was the first person I called. She's my only family, aside from you."

"Then she'll be the baby's godmother."

"And the Professor will be the godfather."

"Agree?"

"Agree."

The next morning, I'm up bright and early. I'd awakened with my arm wrapped around Monica's torso—a hand gently placed on her belly. After quietly getting out of bed, I shower, dress, and kiss the mother and wife-to-be on the forehead before leaving for work.

I walk the streets of San Francisco on a glorious summer day. I'm the first to arrive at The Hall. Within an hour, Mike Gates and Ana and Isabella show up. I ask that they meet me at the bar. Keeping a serious tone, I say, "I have something to tell you guys. Something important."

"Tell me you're not selling Hall," chimes in Mike Gates.

"I'm not selling The Hall," I say, still maintaining an air of seriousness.

Ana and Isabella stare at me while I stare back at them. Finally, at a raised volume, Ana says, "What, Jack?"

I morph from serious to a shit-eating grin, saying, "We're gonna have a baby!"

In unison, we begin to hoot and holler and hug and carry on, acting bat shit crazy. Ana finally asks, "Does this mean you're getting married?"

"Yes. Right here at The Hall in a month. Matty's going to perform the ceremony."

Round two of hooting and hollering and hugging commences. Mike Gates proposes a toast. He pours three shots of chilled Polish vodka and a shot of orange juice. We raise our glasses high in the air as Mike Gates toasts:

"To love, family, friends, good food, drink, and happy baby. Salute."

"Salute!"

FIFTY-SIX

JACK

The following month is a whirlwind. Monica and I are constantly on the go, working and handling multiple priorities over the phone and in person. She's either with my mom or Big Sandy and rarely alone. I'm mostly with Rosenbaum, sometimes with Matty, and often checking in with Ana to make sure I'm doing what a fiancé and father-to-be should be doing. Names for the baby are agreed upon. Neither one of us wanting to know gender until the little tike enters the world.

One Sunday, while we're visiting my mom, the topic of moving into a house versus living in a high-rise apartment comes up. My mom mentions she'd like to hand over the house to us so the grandbaby can grow up in a safe neighborhood, the same neighborhood and house where I was raised. As we warm to the idea, we agree to decide after the baby is born. Mom says, "Take your time, but either way, at some point you're getting the house."

My mom hosts a baby shower for Monica. The invited guests are in short supply. Big Sandy, Ana and Isabella,

Jasmine, —plus two of Monica's employees from The Blue Bean—show up for fun and frivolity. Regardless of the size of the function, Monica can't stop talking about it—surprised as she was by all the kindness.

For my bachelor function, me and the Professor, Mike Gates, and Matty consume a fabulous dinner in a private room at an old-school Italian restaurant out in North Beach. Good food, drink, conversation, and laughs. I'm home before midnight.

One week to go before the big day. We're stoked, both looking forward to getting married and starting a family.

The next week flies by. Before we know it, Saturday at one in the afternoon is staring us in the face. With The Hall decked out in rows of chairs and tables decorated to the nines, Monica and I couldn't be more pleased. Ana has transformed the place from bar/music hall to wedding chapel/reception hall.

Promptly at one, me and Rosenbaum join Matty on stage. Jasmine, poised stage right in front of an organ, begins the wedding theme. All in attendance turn their attention toward the front door. In walks Monica in all her splendor, wearing a simple yet elegant white dress with fresh flowers in her hair. Tears well as my beautiful bride makes her way down the center aisle. She's escorted by Big Sandy, who plays a double role in the ceremony.

Once Monica has safely navigated the ramp and is facing me, Matty begins. In the name of brevity, the wedding ceremony is over in less than twenty minutes.

"I do."

"I do."

Joy!

Now married and giddy, Monica and I and certain family

members and friends retreat through the backroom for additional photos outside. Ana and crew remove the rows of chairs and push the dining tables to their designated spots, setting up for the special meal prepared by Mike Gates and staff. Not shy, the guests make their way over to the bar, where a couple of bartenders work at a clipped pace to keep up with the thirsty throng.

The organ is removed from the stage to make room for the reception band's gear. The band hired for the event is a mini-orchestra named Orch-Light Review, a band highly recommended by Barney Kellogg. The stylish band from Lubbock, Texas, plays a mixture of music from a range of eras.

Once the photo session is done, Monica and I make a return appearance to hobnob with guests and finally sit down to eat before the dancing starts. After an all-day affair, we bow out just before midnight with the festivities still in full swing.

The following morning we're off to the airport, flying to Kauai for a week of walking from lounger to ocean back to lounger. Time screams by and, in the blink of an eye, we find ourselves flying home. Back in San Francisco, we fall into the routine of it all, awaiting the baby's arrival.

Before we know it, we're parents. Parents to a twenty-one-inch, eight-pound baby boy: Sean Pete O'Shea.

Quickly convinced high-rise living isn't infant friendly, we change course and move into my mom's house. She agrees to stay with us for the first two years to dote on her grandchild and play the role of nanny. I'm relieved—my immediate family under the safe confines of the same roof.

Rosenbaum is in full agreement that I maintain my place at *The City Wrap* building. It's close to work, and we'd rather not alter our business arrangement. Monica and I spend an occasional weekend at the old apartment, sometimes with little Sean and sometimes not. My mom also uses it as a getaway for private time and shopping. Matty is given a key to the apartment as well, so he and the mayor can conduct one-on-one meetings.

FIFTY-SEVEN

DONNA O'SHEA

I put little Sean down for a nap, tiptoeing from the bedroom and quietly shutting the door. Once in the kitchen, I make sure I can clearly see the baby on the video monitor while hearing every noise the audio portion emits. Overly cautious, I turn the volume up a notch.

Walking the length of the living room, I prop the front door open to air out the house as an offshore breeze rushes up the avenues. I lock the screen door—unlock it, then lock it again—convincing myself it's locked. Back in the kitchen, I wash and stack the breakfast dishes before making my way over to the hall closet to retrieve the upright vacuum. Starting in the dining room, I vacuum the entire house except for the baby's room. I'll attack that later when the little guy is awake and occupied by adoring parents.

The two bathrooms are next. First, the one in the master bedroom, the room I've given up to the newlyweds. Once finished, I open a window to assist with cross ventilation. Street noises creep in—voices, traffic, outside sounds. Off to the second bathroom.

I start up again, then suddenly stop as I hear something out of the ordinary. Not sure what it is, I check the baby's room, quietly opening the door and peeking inside. Seeing the baby in a deep sleep—his little chest expanding, contracting—I relax and think myself to be a worrywart, gently closing the door and returning to the bathroom. Task complete, I make my way back to the kitchen, washing my hands and again viewing the video monitor.

Coming out of the kitchen, I take several strides before abruptly stopping in my tracks—my momentum causing me to lean forward. All at once I'm startled, scared, pissed off, and ready to scratch her eyes out. "How did you get in here?"

"Now, Donna, that's not a nice way to greet an old friend. Especially a friend with a gun," says Maddie O'Shea, pointing a pistol at me. "You might want to get a better screen door installed."

Staring at the gun and ignoring her smartass comment, I ask, "What do you want, Maddie?"

"Thanks for asking. Jack has what I want. He has until Sunday to drop it off at my house. I will be home from Mass by eight thirty-five both tomorrow and Sunday morning. I will be there the rest of the day, each day. Please let him know that if he continues to ignore his promises something might happen to that baby sleeping in the other room." She points the gun's barrel in that direction. "You've been easy to track, Donna. Easy to keep an eye on. And if it weren't for the baby, you'd already be dead. Call the police and we'll have ourselves a liar's contest; friends simply meeting for a chat. They'll never find the gun and I'll certainly get hold of another if Jack doesn't keep his word."

"I'll let Jack know as soon as you leave, Maddie."

"I know you will. Goodbye for now, and please tell Jack

he better not fuck with me anymore. I'm not playing games." Maddie backs up to the screen door, places the gun in her handbag, and casually leaves the house as if she'd dropped by for tea and biscuits.

I run to the front door and quickly shut and lock it. Pressing my back up against it, I let out a huge sigh of relief before hurrying to the back bedroom to check on the baby. He continues to sleep a baby's sleep. Hustling to the kitchen, I call Jack, never taking my eye off the monitor while quickly explaining the situation, trying not to get emotional. Livid, he says he's on his way home.

By the time Jack arrives, Monica has been there for a good five minutes. He finds us in the kitchen, the baby propped in his mother's lap. More than worried, Monica looks up at Jack and asks, "What do you have that she wants?"

"A letter. My Cousin Sean's suicide letter."

"Are you going to give it to her?"

"I am. I'm pissed off at myself for holding onto it this long."

"Where is it?"

"Locked inside the gun safe in our closet."

"Can I read it?"

"Of course," says Jack, as he goes to get the letter.

Returning to the kitchen, he hands her the letter and she hands him the baby. Monica unfolds the letter and reads it. Finished reading, she says something that surprises me. "I figured as much."

Again, they swap letter and baby as Monica says, "Give it to her on Sunday at church. Do not go to her house. Be smart and safe. All she wants is the letter." Monica stands up and heads for the front door with a cooing baby in her arms. She takes him across the street to the park.

Jack, changing the subject, says, "I'll call a guy tomorrow

who's an expert in home security. I'll get the doors and locks upgraded. Install some cameras."

"Makes sense. That'll make me feel better," I reply.

"It's time for me to stand up to the O'Shea's. Time to get rid of a letter." With that said, he walks away, following in his family's wake.

FIFTY-EIGHT

DAVID O'SHEA

I wake up in pitch blackness, an unnerving lightlessness, with no clue where I'm at. Listening, I hear a mechanical humming coming from beneath me, while also feeling a rolling motion that has to be drawn-out swells. My assumption: I'm on a boat. Probably a ship.

I reach out and feel for a lower level, finding flooring within inches. Twisting around and sitting up, I abruptly introduce my forehead to something hard. Stunned, I crouch and bend forward, cautiously getting down on all fours while slowly breathing in, then out. Pissed at myself for not checking my surroundings better, I gather strained wits and shake the fog from my brain.

Overly cautious, I crawl in one direction, stopping at each fraction of forward movement to feel for anything solid. At last, I touch a barrier—a wall. I scoot up and position my back against it. Assuming I'm in a room, I stand up like a mime rehearsing a slow-motion routine, finally turning around and facing the wall, palms flat and arms extended. I shuffle to my right—three moderate sidesteps—and go from wall to doorframe to door, eventually touching a door handle. Twisting the handle reveals it's locked. I feel for a light switch, find two side by side, and flip one on. The room lights up, a soft-hued red. It's still overpowering to eyes that have only known darkness for who knows how long. Blinking, I turn around to check things out.

After regaining visual clarity, I quickly calculate that I'm being held in a twelve-by-twelve-foot room with wall-mounted bunk beds, a refrigerator positioned underneath a two-door cupboard, and a small sink stationed next to a stainless-steel toilet without a seat, similar to those found in jails. Having to pee like a racehorse, I walk over to the toilet. As I aim—at the verge of release—I realize for the first time that I'm wearing hospital scrubs and socks. When I start to pee, I also notice a bandage on my right arm, a spot of dried blood dotting the middle. The spot reminds me of something, but I can't quite remember what. Finished, I pull up the near-weightless green pants, flush the toilet, and turn around and take a seat on the toilet as if it's a chair.

Looking up, I re-check the room and finally find what I'm looking for. There are four of them . . . cameras, mini domes, each one mounted in upper corners. Also, when I pull on the door there's little movement, if any. The door appears to be reinforced; I'm assuming with a deadbolt lock. Apparently they, whoever they are, don't want me roaming around of my own accord.

Looking for a phone or some type of communication device, I come up empty except for a speaker screen in the ceiling above the sink. I also notice a vent that's much too narrow to fit through and wonder if the ship's designers consciously thought that through. Not trying to overthink things, I open the refrigerator and cupboard and find them fully stocked.

After a quick perusal, I decide to make a sandwich. Finding a single set of plasticware, I assemble a meal. I think about mouthing hello to one of the cameras but decide against it. They will come for me when they're good and ready and not a second before.

After eating and tidying up, I notice the bottom bunk can be lifted and secured to the wall at an angle, creating additional space in the tiny environment. Doing so reveals plastic storage containers that house a set of towels and toiletries and a dozen or so paperback books. Removing the containers and placing the bunk back in its original position, I select a book, situate myself on the bottom bunk, and begin to read. Within minutes, I'm fast asleep in the glowing red room.

I awake rested, not knowing how long I've slept. Thirsty as hell, I grab a bottle of water from the fridge, along with a can of root beer. Downing the water, I start on the soda, and after a few strong pulls, the ice-cold root beer is history, too. I reach across the lower bunk and turn on a mini light located against the back wall. Walking over to the door, I turn off the red lights.

I have no sense of time or the day of the week. Back on the bunk, I take another stab at the paperback. Who knows when I'll hear from another living soul? The smart move is to wait and ignore my wandering mind, disregard the brutal psychology of it all. I'll find out soon enough what's coming my way. But not on my time.

FIFTY-NINE

DAVID O'SHEA

Maybe two days later—leaning over the sink, brushing my teeth—I finally get wind of another human being. At first, I'm not sure what I'm hearing when static leaks into the room. A moment later, through the overhead speaker, a male voice says, "Good morning, David."

I go from slightly bent over to standing straight, offering no verbal response in return. I'm told that in thirty minutes two men will arrive and escort me to another part of the ship. They will bring a pair of flip-flops to be worn in place of socks. Also, after they approach the cabin door, I will be instructed to get on my knees in front of the bottom bunk and to lower my forehead onto the mattress while placing both hands behind my back. Handcuffs will be part of the deal. I'm asked to nod my head in agreement if I understand the instructions given. I nod.

Right on time, the voice chimes in. Once in place, I hear a key go into two locks, unlocking one at a time. My earlier assumption proves right. They enter and approach. I do not turn around to assess, but sense largeness. One of them kneels and handcuffs me. The cuffs are put on by a professional—smoothly, quickly, not too tight, and double locked. Both men guide me to a standing position, turning as we face the open door. I'm right—they're big, muscular, and could easily pass as strongman twins.

Flip-flops are set in front of me. I step into them. After a thorough body search, one of them places a black hood over my head and loosely cinches it at the neck. I take this as a good sign, making it impossible for me to identify most of my surroundings should I be asked about it down the road. We exit the room—one man brushing by me as the lead, the other nudging me from behind to begin walking. So far, their communication is nonverbal. Never once do they utter a single word to me or to each other. I think about the little deaf girl.

We make our way down a passageway, eventually moving up steep companion ladders. I pay attention during the journey that brings us two decks higher—different smells, different sounds. Desperately wanting a glimpse of the outside world, I seriously crave sunlight and fresh air. Arriving at what must be the destination, a large, strong hand grips my left shoulder, administering pressure and causing me to stop. The lead man knocks on a door. In return, someone on the other side says, "Enter." The door opens and I'm ushered inside. The handcuffs are temporarily taken off one wrist and then reattached in front of me. I'm guided into a comfortable chair as the hood is loosened and removed from my head.

I blink while inhaling deeply, now staring at a man sitting behind a modern desk. The dark-tinted glass desktop is bare. The unknown man, dressed in a well-tailored coat and vest, fits the image of top dog for a Fortune 500 company. He's fiftyish but looks ten years younger, with ultra-lean features like those of a welterweight boxer. With piercing hazel eyes that intimidate, he greets me by saying, "Good morning, David. My name is Jonathon. I work for a group of men who are interested in you. But before I get to that, can I get you something to drink? Water? Tea? Coffee?"

I detect a European accent from the man in charge. Just a hint. He speaks proper, educated English, but he's not a Brit and definitely not an American. "Water will do."

Jonathon looks up and one of the guards reaches over to a paneled wall and pulls a lever. A door opens, revealing a full-sized refrigerator. Removing a water, he takes two short strides and hands me the squarish bottle before resuming his original position. I watch as the door shuts on its own, blending in with the wall once again. Unscrewing the cap, I take two quick sips.

Jonathon begins where he left off. "The men I work for had a woman in their employ whose expertise revolved around sensitive projects. She was exceptionally good at her job and considered a valued asset. Her name is not important. But what is important is that you hired her to perform a special service, a service she completed in its entirety. However, no one has heard from her since, and the fee for services rendered has yet to be recovered."

I lean forward and attempt to say something, but I'm met with the raising of a hand and the shaking of Jonathon's head from side to side. Deflated, I fall back into listening mode, never uttering a single syllable.

"There is nothing for you to say to me today, David. Nothing. Tomorrow, however, will be a different day altogether, the day when you are allowed to explain your actions and tell me everything I need to know. When you get back to your cabin, you will find a questionnaire. You will also find a notepad and pen to go along with the questionnaire. Take your time and jot down notes before answering the questions. I want complete, truthful answers. I already know the answers to most of the questions. To a limited few, I do not. However, it is of the utmost importance—and I can't stress this point enough—that you answer each question accurately, completely, and, by all means, honestly. Save your questions, or anything else you'd like to say to me, for tomorrow. Print your answers legibly. Do not consider wasting my time. Thank you, David. Until tomorrow."

The hood drops over my head, the plastic bottle is taken from my hand. I'm raised to my feet, and the handcuffs are once again locked behind my back. Reverse course—the smell of diesel getting stronger during the descent—as I'm led back to my room. Once the door is completely locked (two clicks), I stand up. The questionnaire is resting on the top bunk. I switch on the reading lamp above my bunk and turn the overhead lights off.

I give the questionnaire a thorough read, at last fully understanding my predicament. I'll give them their answers and name names. Reality is, I have no choice. I'll tell them everything. Well, almost everything, as I start writing notes on the legal pad.

SIXTY

DAVID O'SHEA

The following day, I'm given another thirty-minute heads-up before being retrieved. The process repeats: knock-knock, handcuffs, flip-flops, hood. One of the guards asks for the questionnaire. I motion toward the top bunk with my head.

When we leave, instead of making a right turn, we hang a left. We soon descend one level, the thrum of diesel engines becoming more prominent. There's no knocking on doors when we get to where we're going. This time, we simply stop and a lever is raised—metal on metal, scraping. A whoosh of air presses the hood into my face as I hear the groan of a heavy door swinging open.

I'm told to be careful and instructed to step up and over an open hatchway's bottom lip, and to duck slightly to avoid bumping my head. The guards' booted steps echo as we enter what feels like a generous space. I hear the door being shut and secured behind me.

Led an additional few yards before abruptly stopping, I'm told to step out of my flip-flops and pants, as the tie around my waist is loosened and the lightweight cloth drops to the floor. The handcuffs and hood are removed, along with my shirt. The two guards lift my naked body off the deck in a sitting position and place me in a suspended cage . . . the wire mesh door is shut and locked.

I find myself in a cube, maybe eight-foot square. The strong, thick, metal wire is uncomfortable on exposed skin, muscle, bone. I notice multiple cables extending from the cage to the cargo hold overhead. The weight distribution is even, making it relatively easy to crawl to the center of the cage without rocking in any one direction.

Sitting with my knees close to my chest, I lock eyes with Jonathon. He sits outside the cage in a foldup chair, wearing a different suit. Another man is present, someone I've never seen before, sitting in front of a portable desk and a razor-thin laptop. Holding the questionnaire in his hand, Jonathon looks away and watches as the two guards exit the spacious cargo hold.

Jonathon opens with, "Good morning, David." I remain silent. Jonathon's eyes settle on the questionnaire, on my written answers. Slowly, he gazes up at me and says, "It appears you were honest and complete with most of your answers. The problem you now face is that I gave you fair warning. I specifically recall asking you to be honest, accurate, and complete with all your answers. I will have to prove to you that I do not bluff. The gentleman to my right has control over electrical currents that can be sent throughout every millimeter of the metal cage you're sitting in. With a flick of the finger, he can bring you to your knees, your back, your stomach, or whatever position you may find yourself in as you bounce and skip and scream for him to stop the madness."

"That won't be necess—

"Shut up! You are in no position to speak to me. I will tell you when you can speak."

With that said, Jonathon says something to the other man in another language. I think it to be Czech or Polish or Russian. But what I think doesn't matter in the slightest, because all stray thoughts are ripped from my consciousness when the unnamed man presses a key on the laptop.

The cage becomes a living hell as electricity sweeps in and around and begins doing what it's designed to do. I shoot off the cage floor, making sounds I've never made before—convulsing as if having a seizure—bouncing off the cage floor and walls and screaming while losing complete control of my bladder and bowel functions. After a brutal sample of what's to come if I entertain more thoughts of untruths, I find myself lying on my side, gasping for breath. I look out at the well-dressed man who's observing me as if attending a Broadway play.

Spitting through the bottom of the cage, I watch as a long strand of blood, saliva, and snot drops to the deck. I stay put, catching my breath, feeling the aches and pains of newly acquired injuries. I decide to be honest.

It hurts as I sit up. Defeated, I say, "What do you want to know?"

"That, David, is an excellent change in attitude," replies Jonathon. "Let us get to the truth. I'm going to run through your answers. If I read something that is accurate, please reply with a simple yes. If I read something that is not accurate, or needs further explanation, please elaborate. Shall we?"

He begins. "After hiring the woman in question and paying the upfront fee of one-hundred-thousand dollars, did she perform the agreed-upon job to your satisfaction?"

"Yes."

"She then ended up missing. You say that a Mr. Matthew Marshall, a member of the San Francisco police department, killed her."

"Yes."

"You did not have her killed?"

"No. Marshall killed her to protect his cousin. The two women were having an affair, an affair that wasn't going to end well for his cousin."

"Really? That's the truth?"

"Yes."

"But Marshall didn't take any money. He was protecting his family, not ripping off a contract killer. Is this accurate?"

"Yes."

"But you wrote down that Marshall killed her for the money. Is that not true?"

"It's not true. After Marshall took care of your employee, my guy searched the house and found the money. All of it. We split it fifty-fifty."

"What guy?"

"Neil Stanza."

"And he also works for the San Francisco police department?"

"Not anymore. He's dead. Marshall took care of him, too."

"Where is the other half of the money?"

"You'd have to ask his wife. But I seriously doubt she knows. They didn't have a good marriage, and he didn't share much with her. If she found it, it's because she accidentally stumbled across it after he died."

Jonathon gives me a long, intense stare with those piercing eyes. "I believe you. Where is your share of the money?"

"In an account with my other money."

"How much?"

"Seven-hundred-thousand dollars, give or take."

"Who has access to it?"

"Just me."

"Give me the bank name, account number, and access code."

I recite the requested information from memory. The man at the laptop pulls out a cell phone and makes a call, speaking in a foreign language to whoever's on the other end. We sit in silence. Finally, the laptop man's cell phone chirps. He answers, listens, and clicks off. He appears to fill Jonathon in, who eventually nods before directing his attention back to me. I'm guessing that my money is gone . . . *no honor among thieves*.

Jonathon asks, "If you were Neil Stanza, where would you hide the money?"

"Knowing Neil, it's probably in his attic. He keeps cash stored up there in ammo boxes. Or he used to."

"Good to know. Do you have any questions for me?"

"Why are you holding me responsible for her death? I didn't kill her."

"That is an easy question to answer. You were responsible for her safety while she was in San Francisco. You failed. Have a nice afterlife, David."

Jonathon and the other man stand up and leave. All lights are turned off. Back in complete darkness, I contemplate death. I contemplate electricity.

What is surely hours later, I'm brought to my senses by a loud noise and the sun's brightness as a section of the cargo hold overhead opens up to the sky. I instantly feel warmth and humidity rush in. I inhale deeply. The freighter is no longer motoring in any one direction; it rests idle, lightly swaying in barely an ocean swell.

The ship's crane lifts away the upper cargo hatch. Two deckhands enter the hold and begin lowering the suspended cage onto a sturdy dolly after disconnecting a series of cables and wires. A hose spewing chilly water is placed through the top of the cage. Just prior to walking away for a smoke break, one of the deckhands says, "Sir, we are gentlemen. Please have a drink of water and wash yourself."

With their backs to the cage, I take a long drink of fresh water and then use the hose as a shower, washing away grime and sweat and nastiness. I flash back to my youth, remembering a time when I was a little boy, feeling sorry for myself.

Once the hose is removed, the cage is easily rolled to a position underneath the large opening. The crane's reaching arm is centered above it. A strong cable and hook lower, stopping mere inches from the cage. A deckhand climbs atop the cage and connects the crane's hook to a large U-bolt fastened to an O-ring centered at the top of the cage. Task complete, the deckhand climbs down and his partner loops a line through the cage to keep it steady as it lifts off the deck. Up it goes. Slow, controlled. Clearing the hatch and now above deck, the guiding deckhand releases one end of the rope. The open end passes through the cage and falls inside the cargo hold. With the crane sweeping to its left, I peer up at a clear blue sky.

As the cage rests on the main deck, the crane's hook is disconnected and the U-bolt unfastened and removed. In its place, a cable is threaded through the O-ring—maybe six feet in length, with built-in eyelets at each end and an odd-looking turnbuckle fixed off-center. Both eyelets are inserted into the crane's hook.

With the crew at a distance, the cage lifts up and away.

Once past the ship's side rail, the crane continues left another thirty feet until the cage is suspended over water. The cage is slowly lowered to the ocean surface. For the first time in my life I feel and understand despair.

The smallish freighter floats in the middle of a calm ocean. The nearest slice of land is nowhere to be seen, nor are other ships, airplanes, even clouds. Jonathon stands at the ship's rail, looking out at the cage as it dips but an inch into the water. I sit upright and look straight ahead, making fleeting eye contact with him.

Jonathon has a black object the size of a TV remote in his right hand. I may have begged for the electricity to stop, for the pain to stop, but I will not beg for my life. With a slight hand movement, the strong cable attached to the crane's hook disconnects at the turnbuckle and the cage slides into waiting water.

Like my son, I will die naked and alone in the ocean.

SIXTY-ONE

JACK

I leave the house at four, heading for the ocean on a dark, dreary Sunday morning—wetsuit half on, goggles dangling around my neck. After a quick stretch on a towel unraveled in the sand, I methodically make my way into the cold water and up to the first set of breakers. Jumping up, the small waves hit me at waist level. The second set is coming in higher, so under I go as heavy water passes overhead. Surfacing, I swim west beyond the waves, two hundred yards or so, before turning left and swimming south for roughly thirty minutes. I keep track of time with a glowing, water-resistant timepiece. Time's up. I turn around and swim back. Walking from the ocean, I grab my towel, a warm shower on my mind.

Leaving the house again just before six a.m., I drive in the direction of Noe Valley, a neighborhood nestled in the center of the city. I'm in search of a diner, just the right greasy spoon that serves up a hearty breakfast. I'm not in a hurry and plan to enter the church fifteen minutes after the service begins. But first I do a drive-by, cruising past the church and my aunt's house. With that out of the way, I circle out in a five-block radius until I find what I'm looking for. There it is—a red neon *Open* sign hanging in the window. I hustle a parking space a block away before jog-walking back to Paul's Pancake Palace. How can I go wrong with a place with that name?

Inside, I look around before deciding to sit at the counter. The diner has a neighborhood feel to it. A guy with a sewn-on nametag that reads *Paul* asks if I'm ready to order. I start with a cup of steaming black coffee while ordering the biggest stack of pancakes I can get, along with fresh strawberries and butter and maple syrup. Paul says, "Coming right up."

Once I've consumed half a cup of coffee and the legal drug starts to kick in, I grab a stray copy of the morning *Chronicle* and read an article about my uncle on page four of the city section. The article is narrow in scope, speculating that David O'Shea could be living in South America with a load of stolen money and hired help at the ready. The writer even quotes an anonymous source who says a distant relative saw O'Shea in a bar in Venezuela—a voluptuous model hanging on his arm. Highly doubtful, I conclude, as a ginormous stack of buckwheat pancakes is slid onto the counter in front of me. A mound of carbs. I gobble them up in record time before getting a refill on my coffee.

Leaving the diner, I drive over to the church and find a parking space less than a block away. It's seven thirty-five; no rush, stay put a few minutes. Not surprisingly, I'm a little nervous. I remove the letter from the envelope and give it a final read. Finished reading, a pang of unrest registers deep in my belly. I get out of the car and take a short walk in an attempt to settle my nerves.

Let's do this, I think, as I circle back and take the steps two at a time and enter the church's vestibule. Not feeling

Catholic, I ignore the holy water and walk over to a door leading directly inside. I push the door open a few inches and peer in. It's an old rectangular-shaped church with wooden pews on the left and right and a center aisle separating the two. The business of saving souls is slow during early morning Mass. I count nine people on the right, but my aunt is not one of them. Pushing the door open wider, I look at the pews on the left. I scan from front to back, quickly discerning the left side has fewer people than the right. I wonder if she's a no-show. Farther down, I finally spot her. She's wearing all black, including a hat and veil. Old school.

I open the door and step inside. Making as little noise as possible, I gently guide the door shut. I'm standing less than a half-dozen pews directly behind her. Positioned at the far right, she's the only person in her row. Easy in, easy out for communion, and a quick escape once the service ends.

I make my approach from a side aisle on her left. She doesn't notice when I enter the row, but certainly feels my presence when I slide her way on polished wood—even more so when our shoulders touch. With the envelope in my right hand, I reach out and drop it in her lap as the man in the funny robe spews rehearsed nonsense from the pulpit. Sit, kneel, stand, repeat practiced words, cross yourself.

Maddie looks at the letter lying in her lap, then looks straight ahead. Isolated from the rest of the sparse congregation, Maddie, in a low tone, says, "I know you think you know who I am and what I am, Jack. But you don't know me. Bad people are capable of doing good things, and good people are capable of doing despicable things, depending on their circumstances and needs. Most people rarely know their true selves. But we can all be guided to do certain things that are inherently in us, whether we acknowledge them or not." Turning toward me, she adds, "Fuck you, Jack. Fuck you and your judgments and the judgments of your family and friends."

We're silent as the priest continues with the service, his trained participants following along. Tired of the silence, I finally say, "You must think I'm either dumb or blind, but I definitely think you're crazy."

"How crazy is crazy when crazy speaks the truth, Jack?"

"Not sure what that means, Maddie. I came here to give you a letter and to tell you to stay away from my family. I'm not interested in your take on a deplorable situation regarding your child. A child you brought into this world. Right now, I just want to get the hell out of this church and as far away from you as possible."

"Try not to act like an infant, Jack. Life can be wicked at times. Now run along and leave me alone."

I remain still, speechless. My heart thumps as if ready to explode. I take a deep breath, hold it, and let it out slow—calming myself. Finally, I lean in, whispering, "Mothers and fathers shouldn't fuck their children."

Her entire body tenses as if ready to pounce, fight, rage. But then, just as suddenly, she relaxes, almost limp-like, before standing with the rest of the congregation as if I'm not even there.

Time to make my move. I slide to the left, stand up, and hustle to the end of the pew, hanging a quick left. At the back of the church, I make another left and eventually a hard right through the door in which I'd entered. Once back in the vestibule, breathing becomes difficult, like I'm suffocating.

Bursting through the last set of doors, I inhale deeply, glad to be breathing city air and not the restricted air of false worship and lies. I feel a sense of relief, having confronted my past by saying what needed to be said. At the very least, I owed Sean that much. Owed myself and my family, too.

When I arrive home, I walk into a house filled with the smells of breakfast and a baby. Relieving Monica of the little tyke, I spin around the kitchen until he begins to laugh. I soon slow my roll so neither one of us pukes.

Monica asks, "How'd it go?"

"It went how it should have gone. She has the letter. It's over."

My mom walks in and asks the identical question. With the patience of Job, I repeat myself. Monica smiles. The baby drools. And my mom says, "Good. Then it's over."

Our Sunday plays out like it always does—family, laughs, love, food, gratitude. But we're all kidding ourselves, whether we know it or not.

I doubt it's over. Not yet anyway.

250

JOHN ALLEN MACHADO

SIXTY-TWO

JASMINE

I stand in the wings, watching as the veteran musician wows the crowd with riff after riff on his alto sax. I'd been offered the opportunity to fly to Seattle and open for the well-known jazzman. Jumping at the opportunity, I caught a last-minute flight up to the Emerald City to play two shows in front of three-thousand people at a restored downtown theater.

After the show, I'm invited to a private after-hours function. I quickly accept, hanging with the main group of musicians heading over. On the way up to the penthouse—in a smoked-glass elevator at a swank hotel—the band's bass player makes mention that what awaits us in the penthouse is a who's who of financial support for the West Coast jazz scene. "So remember," he adds, "no shoot'n 'H' in the bathroom." Everyone breaks out laughing as we arrive at the party in the sky, thirty-four floors high.

They treat us like royalty, which, at first, seems surreal. Exchanging pleasantries with strangers and thanking them for their kind words, I slowly wind my way over to the bar and order a glass of chilled Russian vodka with a lemon twist. After receiving my drink, I smile at the bartender and place a twenty-dollar bill in the tip jar. Turning around, I come face to face with a handsome man in an elegant chocolate-brown suit with silver pinstripes.

"I see you like good vodka," says the stranger. "You have excellent taste in classical music as well."

"Thank you. My early training focused more on classical than jazz. I'm sorry for being rude. I'm Jasmine," I say, extending a hand.

The unfamiliar man shakes my hand and says, "I know who you are, and I should be the one apologizing for my lack of manners. My friends and close business associates call me Jonathon. It is a pleasure to finally meet you."

"It's nice to meet you, too. You like classical music?" I ask.

"I do, and also jazz. You were wonderful tonight, as was Sonny Tone and his band."

"I thought they were great as well. I'd never heard Sonny play live before tonight. But I've listened to his older stuff from my father's collection."

"Believe it not, I saw your father perform in Europe in my youth. Like I said, I'm a fan of jazz and John Marshall has been a part of my musical collection for decades."

"That is so kind of you to say. I listen to my dad's music often. He's still my main inspiration. He means everything to me. He's still with me."

"I can tell that family is important to you," says the man with striking hazel eyes. "It is important to me as well. I will now leave you to the others. I do not want to be selfish. That's not true. I do want to be selfish, but I won't be. Just remember, you have a loyal fan named Jonathon and I will continue to follow your career closely. Just like I did with your father, your mentor. Until next time, cheers!"

We touch glasses and I smile and thank my handsome devotee. As he walks away, a throng of new admirers fill the void. He touched my heart with the mention of seeing my father perform live.

The rest of the night is filled with me talking to way too many people. I'm smart, though, switching from vodka to water after two cocktails. The bartender I'd tipped earlier has my back, serving me water cocktails disguised as vodka. No one's the wiser. I still have another performance and need to be at my best in front of eager fans primed for The Sonny Tone Project.

Upon entering the green room the next evening, I find two-dozen long-stemmed white roses awaiting me. There's a card attached. As I open it, something falls to the floor. I reach down and pick it up. A ticket stub from a John Marshall concert in Hamburg, Germany, on October 2, 1977. I read the card, tearing up after the first line: Play tonight with your father in your heart. He was the musician who turned me on to a music that is best left unexplained. John Marshall played from his heart. He moved me. Best regards, Jonathon.

I play on another level . . . an elevated plane. My hands float across the keys as I feel each and every note as if they all have meaning—because they do. I sing from my soul. When finished, I'm exhausted. My father had mentioned this feeling long ago, a feeling I'm experiencing for the first time. I now get it.

The crowd roars.

SIXTY-THREE

JAVIER MONTOYA

The widow Stanza vowed to change her ways the second she realized her husband was dead. She inherited a partial pension, funds from a life insurance policy, and a house in San Francisco free and clear of a monthly mortgage. Life was about to go from bland to spicy. But Mrs. Stanza's newfound commitment only took place in her mind. With the exception of some motivational fantasies, she never committed to action, never thought to actually do something about her listless situation. Mrs. Stanza's main comfort foods remained diazepam and vodka, with a dash of cranberry juice for coloring.

JAVIER MONTOYA

In bed and halfway to oblivion, there's no way she hears me as I root around in the attic above the garage. My boss was right, I have no problem finding the dark green ammo boxes. There they stand, twenty-one of them, lined up in a neat row on a sheet of plywood butted up against a far wall. From left to right, ammo box eight has fifty-thousand dollars in hundred-dollar bills tucked snugly inside. Ammo box seventeen catches me by surprise, with twenty-seven-thousand dollars in fifties and hundreds nestled in its confines.

I'm pleased with the additional find. I'll be taking more money than anticipated back to the boss. However, I'm more excited about what's inside the other nineteen boxes because they contain enough ammo and explosives to take out an entire city block.

I combine the money into one box. After giving it some serious thought, I roll the dice, transporting the money and all the other boxes down to the garage—one at a time. Careful not to make any undue noise that might alert the drunken widow, I'm relieved when I hear her screaming at her television set, apparently upset with a game show contestant. More important, though, I don't want what's inside the containers to explode. That would not make the boss happy.

I carry the ammo boxes from the garage to a parked van, treating the containers like fragile china being moved from glass shelf to glass shelf. Driving away satisfied but slightly nervous, I cautiously avoid bumps and potholes on the drive back to the hotel.

The following day, there's a knock on my door. It takes me but a fraction of a second to open up. There stand Jonathon and his lovely assistant, Tasha. Nineteen of the twenty containers are neatly positioned on the hotel bed, the twentieth held in my arms like a precious baby. I happily hand it over to Jonathon.

After opening the container and peering inside, Jonathon fingers a bundle of money before looking up and raising his eyebrows.

"Seventy-seven thousand dollars. Fifty grand in one box and twenty-seven in the other. And let me apologize up front, boss. As you can see, I also brought back the rest of the boxes. They contain ammo and explosives. You could blow up a skyscraper with what's inside them."

"Javier, you made a decision and it has yet to jeopardize our objective. We'll recap later. Call Reuben and have him come over straightaway and thoroughly inspect the contents of each box to determine if what's inside is safe or not. Reuben will properly handle the explosives. When you are finished assisting him, come up to my suite."

"You got it, boss."

I break out my cell phone and make the call.

Jonathon and Tasha and the money head for the thirty-ninth floor, to the largest suite in the hotel.

Two hours later, Tasha greets me at the door of the luxurious suite. She guides me into a sparsely furnished room where Jonathon sits behind a desk, a smart phone held to his ear. I look out at multiple city vistas—three different windows, three different directions.

Ending his call, Jonathon asks if everything has been taken care of. I say, "Yes," adding that Reuben was extremely happy with the inventory inside the boxes. Jonathon stands and walks over, carrying a stack of cash. He hands it to me.

"Consider this a bonus for your efforts and honesty."

I gladly take the money.

But before I can say a word, Jonathon beats me to the punch. "If those explosives had been unsafe, had they detonated for whatever reason, we would've had an entirely different situation on our hands. In the future, don't take that risk. If you ever find yourself in a similar predicament, simply stay the course and do not vary from the agreed-upon plan. If we had the opportunity to repeat yesterday's activities, you would have returned with the money and only the money. Remember, we stick with the plan at all times. We can always devise additional plans if necessary. Any questions?"

"No questions, boss. I won't screw up again. Thank you for the bonus."

"Javier, you didn't screw up. I admire your hard work and integrity. That means more to me than a tactical lapse in judgment. What's done is done and everything worked out. Just don't do it again. Take the rest of the day off and thank you."

SIXTY-FOUR

MADDIE O'SHEA

I receive communion and return to an isolated pew. As the service winds down, I stay in my seat, waiting while the other congregants file from the church. Alone, I make my way out a side exit, avoiding the huddle at the front of the church as I walk directly home.

First thing, I run a bath, placing soap and shampoo and candles at tub's edge. When the bathtub is nearly two-thirds full, I turn the water off and check the temperature with hesitant fingertips. I'll let it cool down a bit before entering. After lighting the candles, I go into my bedroom.

I undress, folding, then putting away clothes. Naked, I ease into a chair next to the bed and read Sean's letter from beginning to end. Gripping the paper and wanting to scream, I watch white knuckles regain color as I recover self-control. I stand up and march to the den, placing the letter in the shredder, watching as it disappears.

Removing the top of the shredder, I grab the container and head out to the garage and dump the confetti-like aftermath in a metal bucket. After searching through a cabinet, I remove a box of matches and strike a single matchstick, taking in the smell of sulfur and liking it. I light the bucket's contents on fire and, within seconds, watch as paper is reduced to smoke and ashes. I dump what's left into the utility sink and wash it down the drain. Adding a little water to the bucket, I swish it around before placing the bucket upside-down, the muck slowly trickling away. Task complete.

Returning to the bathroom, I cautiously step into the waiting water. After settling in, I completely submerge, staying under until it feels uncomfortable. Coming up for air, I focus on ceiling etchings while hovering in liquid heat.

I rest for a brief period before thoroughly washing. Getting out of the tub, I release the stopper; cloudy water swirling away. Clean and calm, I'm ready to get on with it.

Parking myself on the toilet, I smoke a cigarette for the first time in over twenty years, enjoying every inhale and exhale before dropping the butt and spent match between my legs. With that out of the way, I wash my hands before flossing and brushing my teeth.

Removing a small bottle from the medicine cabinet, I return to the bedroom and place it on my pillow. Walking back to the kitchen, I get a bottle from the freezer and a tall drinking glass from a cupboard. I walk the entire house, ensuring order.

Satisfied, I head to the bedroom with a coaster, a hand towel, a bottle, and a glass. I sit on the bed and fill the pint glass within an inch of the rim with chilled French vodka. I reach for the tinted bottle of Phenobarbital resting on my pillow, remove the cap, and tap pills into an open hand—the exact researched amount, plus one more to remove all doubt.

I put the pills in my mouth. Bottoms up! With the glass now empty, I wipe clean the top of the nightstand and place the pill bottle in the glass before setting the glass on the coaster. Stretching out naked on the bed, just prior to falling asleep, I think, *Fuck suicide notes.*

Maddie O'Shea was discovered by two patrol cops the following week, three days after the fact. A concerned neighbor dialed 911 when she noticed Maddie hadn't gone to church for several days. A half hour later, after peering through a bedroom window, one cop looked at another cop and said, "Kick in the door."

Her death provided fodder for the local news affiliates for about a week. The recent suicide dredged up the old suicide, which dredged up the whereabouts of the missing chief. But those stories soon vanished once the local baseball star tested positive for performance-enhancing drugs.

There was no official funeral, but Donna and Jack attended a small service arranged by members of Maddie's parish. They were late to arrive, sitting in a back row and wishing they hadn't come. Less than twenty people showed, with scattered groupings sitting at considerable distances from one another while avoiding eye contact. Donna and Jack were the first to leave once the service concluded.

As he left the church, Jack felt like a jerk, the stench of hypocrisy oozing from guilty pores. Contemplating dead relatives brought on an uneasiness, an emptiness . . . nothing close to good. Oddly, though, he felt a twinge of forgiveness.

On the drive home, Donna and Jack exchanged small talk. After parking the car in the garage, they sat in silence. Neither one had anything to say. Several minutes in, Donna placed a hand on Jack's hand and said it didn't need to be discussed anymore.

It truly was over.

EPILOGUE

JACK

My wife told me a story in a park one afternoon. A story recalled from a time before we knew each other.

Still new to San Francisco, she'd ventured over to the orange industrial behemoth on a cold winter morning—The Golden Gate Bridge. She said strolling out on the bridge walkway induced excitement, an anticipated thrill, like a child stepping into the exposed front car of a rollercoaster for the first time. She'd walked across bridges in New York City many a time, but none like this, she told me, with its monumental presence peering in at the bay while its opposite face looks out across a vast ocean.

Walking its length, she said she stopped on the other side, taking in the limited view, enveloped by mist and wind and layers of smoky fog. In no hurry whatsoever, she took her time—all senses tingling—before beginning the journey back and viewing the limited sights from a different perspective. As she passed mid-span, she stopped and looked to her right, out to a hidden ocean. There were splintered breaks in a wall of fog as several rays of light fought through, playing illusionary tricks. She said she was temporarily transfixed, caught up in nature's radiant show.

With the light show dwindling, she turned toward the walkway. Someone approached—a young man disrobing. First his checkered Vans, one at a time as he continued on barefoot; next, a long-sleeved shirt, light blue, pressed; and finally undoing the button fly on faded jeans as they dropped to the walkway while he stepped out and away, leaving strewn garments in his wake.

She remembered they briefly locked eyes. His eyes like that of her late uncle's—eyes of the damaged.

She couldn't help but mention his skin—bronze, unblemished, taut.

Without warning, he veered away. His movements were smooth, appearing effortless. An athlete, easily vaulting the railing and flying away.

She wondered if he had a family, learning later that he did. Unlike a childhood friend who you haven't seen in years and can't quite recall their name, she never forgot his. Having never said a word to each other, having spent but moments together on a foggy bridge, she couldn't drive him from her mind.

For years, a reoccurring thought entered her mind at the oddest of times. It soon vanished after I handed her a letter. A letter left for me by my cousin. Her thought was this: *I would venture to guess that the reason most people mistreat other people is in direct correlation to their own damaged self.*

Time floated by. Life happened. A contented pattern formed, then a drastic change occurred. Life grew inside her. When she least expected change, change arrived. The baby came and she loved him instantly.

At some point it dawned on her that the man on the bridge was a saint. A true saint. I'm not talking about some voting process to determine sainthood. I'm referring to everyday saints who walk among us, yet go undetected by most, if not by all.

We named our baby after that saint. Sean is Little Sean's uncle. A nephew not to be met. An uncle to learn about, to be remembered. They would've loved each other.

Our baby, Sean, on the other hand, will be loved and protected. We owe him that.